I0685252

The Player Next Door

The Player Next Door

KATHY LYONS

This book is a work of fiction. Names, characters, places, and incidents
are the product of the author's imagination or are used fictitiously.
Any resemblance to actual events, locales, or persons, living or dead, is
coincidental.

Copyright © 2015 by Kathy Lyons. All rights reserved, including the
right to reproduce, distribute, or transmit in any form or by any means.
For information regarding subsidiary rights, please contact the Publisher.

Entangled Publishing, LLC
2614 South Timberline Road
Suite 105, PMB 159
Fort Collins, CO 80525
rights@entangledpublishing.com

Lovestruck is an imprint of Entangled Publishing, LLC.

Edited by Liz Pelletier
Cover design by Bree Archer
Cover photography by SurfUpVector/Getty Images

Manufactured in the United States of America

First Edition July 2015

The Entangled team is amazing. Liz P is a star well beyond that. Thank you all. I could never have done this without you.

Chapter One

It was a sushi cookbook that ended Tori William's five-year relationship with Edward. They were at a small bookstore that served hot chocolate and brought in acoustic guitar musicians when Tori saw the thing. She thought the cover image was clever—a dragon roll curving around wasabi and ginger made to look like a knight on an orange steed.

She smiled at the picture. Edward had taught her not to laugh. He said her sense of humor was often inappropriate and so she smiled rather than chuckled. Grinned rather than laughed. It was the best she could do and he had pronounced that better than nothing.

So she smiled at the picture and held the book up for him to see.

He looked up from his tea and scoffed. "As if you could cook even raw food without poisoning yourself."

"What?" It took her a moment to understand him as she had just seen another book over his shoulder featuring a cute kitten in a teacup. Kittens always distracted her.

"That's raw food, Tori. It takes a special grade meat and

careful monitoring to make sure it doesn't go bad. You'd poison yourself."

She looked back at the dragon vs. knight picture. She hadn't even noticed it was a how-to book. And at that moment, she decided to be irrational and argue.

"I'm an intelligent woman with a PhD," she said in her most prim teacher voice. "Of course I could make sushi without killing anyone."

"I suppose food poisoning isn't necessarily fatal."

"I'm buying this book," she said, suddenly thinking of all the money they would save on sushi if she made it rather than purchased it from their favorite organic Japanese restaurant.

"If you must," he said, going back to his tea and a book on the gruesome death of a pair of foolish mountain climbers. "But I'm not going to eat it."

That was the end of their argument. He'd pronounced the final word and looked back to his own book. It didn't help that he was probably right. She had no true interest in making sushi and was well known for getting distracted while… Well, while doing anything. It was how she was made, and Edward always said it was charming in a rare, overbred toy dog kind of way. She could never survive alone in the wild, according to him, but he appreciated having a purpose in life as her owner.

He never actually said *owner*. He wasn't that stupid. But her sister had made that joke just last week at Aunt Mabel's funeral, and the idea had festered in Tori's thoughts.

"I bought Aunt Mabel's house," Tori said, not intending the words to come out, but then that often happened. Words slipped out while her mind was busy elsewhere.

Edward didn't look up. "You *inherited* it, Tori."

Actually, what she meant is that she paid all the taxes and the mortgage on it. The place was hers now, free and clear.

Meanwhile, Edward wasn't done instructing her on what to do. "Did you contact Georgie? He could use the commission on selling the house, and though that rat trap isn't worth much, it's in a great area."

"No," she admitted, a groundswell of emotions building inside her. She didn't get stirred up by much—she was too easily distracted—but when a storm finally broke, it tended to blow her entire life around.

Meanwhile, Edward set his teacup down with an audible click. It was a clear sign that he was out of patience with her. "Really, Tori, you can't let this just hang out there—a death trap of a house with no one living in it. I'm too busy with the semester ending to take care of this for you. Just call Georgie and have done with it. Some sucker will buy it and with a quick closing we can have a tidy sum within a couple months."

"Can we?" she said, her words sharp and cold. They were like lightning flashes of fury, but he was too caught up in his own irritation to notice. Even when she tossed out the warning shot, "I believe it's *my* inheritance."

"Yes, yes, of course. But we've been talking about buying a boat to sail on Lake Michigan."

No, he'd been talking about that. Tori had no special love of things nautical. No particular hatred either, but it seemed to her that she ought to get some fun out of spending that much money.

"I thought we'd go on safari instead." She'd always wanted to do that.

He frowned, clearly thinking of the possibility. "I suppose a quick trip could be fun. But we'd have to get shots. You know how you hate those."

She nodded. She did hate shots, though she'd suffer through them to go on safari. She had a secret love of African music but it gave Edward a headache.

"You're right," she finally said as she lifted up the book. "No safari."

"Good—"

"I'm going to move into Aunt Mabel's house." She spoke it so calmly that it took a moment for her to realize that here was that storm of emotions bursting through her. Fury had such a grip on her that it had taken over the bulk of her body, making decisions and speaking them out loud while the rational part of her mind was relegated to a tiny shocked corner. Which was weird because she wasn't even shaking and her voice sounded completely rational. But she was furious. She had to be, otherwise what she said made no sense.

Meanwhile, Edward's head whipped around to stare directly at her, his expression darkening into an angry scowl. "Don't be ridiculous. I'm not going to live in that ramshackle place."

She grinned. "I know." Then she walked away and bought her how-to book on sushi.

...

Mike Giamaria jerked in alarm, his only thought: *WTF?*

He'd been out for his third run of the day, enjoying himself as he zipped through Evanston, IL without being followed by the paparazzi. It was a pretty place as suburbia went, and he liked seeing chalk drawings on the sidewalk, a couple fat family dogs snoozing in the shade, and a woman dangling upside down from her roof.

That was when he jerked to a stop.

A woman—blonde and slender—swaying upside down from the roof. One foot was caught in the gutter, but the rest of her was hanging by a thin nylon rope tied to the chimney. She'd looped the cord through the belt loops of her jean cutoffs. Her T-shirt had drifted up to her nose, and while he watched, she stripped the thing off and let it drop lazily to the ground—another good ten feet below her.

He immediately started cataloguing thoughts. First the

assets: creamy white skin, pink bra with a torn piece of lace, and a nice slender torso. Nice cleavage, he thought, even as his mind was racing through the cons. A too-thin nylon rope pulled taut, a ten-plus foot drop, and soft dirt that would still break her neck when she fell.

Holy shit, she was going to die.

That's when his feet started moving again. He easily cleared the package of roofing tiles on the ground. Had she been roofing? Then he leaped over the sickly looking hedge to reach her side.

"Stay calm. I'm here," he said.

Damn, she was too quiet. No hysterics, no screams. Had she fainted? He came up right underneath her, accidentally stepping on her dropped tee. Her head was tilted and her eyes widened in surprise when he came into view.

"Oh hello," she said, her voice surprisingly cheerful. "I didn't see you there."

"Too busy taking a header?" he asked.

But she just frowned as she popped earbuds out of her ears. He could hear the rapid beat of drums, loud and clear. "Sorry. What did you say?"

"Just stay calm," he repeated, though she seemed bizarrely casual. He reached out to steady her, his hands settling on her shoulders even though they practically itched to slide over to her generous tits. The thought wasn't appropriate, but he was a guy after all, and he wasn't immune to the sight.

He waited a beat to refocus his thoughts. Besides, it was best to get over the sudden recognition and starstruck gibbering now. After all, he was a superstar athlete for the Knicks, recognizable even here in Chicagoland. After she'd calmed down, they could move on to deal with the situation.

But nothing happened. He'd flipped his hoodie back so she was staring full at his face. She just looked at him, her expression bizarrely serene.

Okay. So maybe she didn't recognize people upside down. Or maybe she was a little more freaked out than she let on. Her jaw was rigid in the way of someone holding back fear while remaining outwardly calm. Either way, he had to get her down from there.

"Where's the ladder?" he asked. Even with his busted shoulder, he could probably haul her up. But he had to get on top of the roof first.

"My car's a Prius."

"What?"

She frowned at him, then explained with a slow, patient voice. "No ladder. It was too big for my car."

Ah. Right. He'd seen the powder blue thing in the driveway. But… "How'd you get up there?"

She gestured with her arm, the motion making her sway such that her strawberry blond ponytail seemed to spin as she twisted. "Tree."

He looked into the backyard where a dying locust tree had overgrown the roof. Sure it would be an easy climb for a kid, but he wouldn't want to carry roofing tiles up there. Those things were damned heavy. And sure enough, there was another spilled package of tiles on the ground.

Jesus. "Okay. I'll climb the tree."

She twisted back to look at him. Bright blue eyes the color of her car caught his gaze. "Okay. But there's no need."

"You're about to plunge to your death." He wouldn't usually say something like that. One mention of falling and his sisters would have descended into hysterics, but this woman seemed practically blasé. Maybe she'd hit her head and was concussed. That would explain a lot.

She smiled, and he was momentarily startled by the charming sight of her slightly crooked teeth. "Don't be silly. I have everything under control." Then she winked at him. "And if I fall, you can be heroic and catch me."

Things were very much *not* under control, but he recognized the stubborn set to her jaw even if she was hanging upside down. She was an I-can-do-it-myself girl. He had a couple nieces who were masters of that particular mindset, foolish though it was.

"Look, how about I just come up there and—"

"I'm fine," she called. "I've been working out the details." She sounded like she was convincing herself. Then she proved that she was completely nuts. She used her foot—the one that had caught on the gutter and stopped the worst of her fall—and kicked off. While he stood there in slack-jawed astonishment, she started swinging back and forth, kicking off the roof when she could and reaching out for the gutter with her free hand.

He gave her points for innovation, but no way would the gutter hold her weight. It would break off. Plus, she didn't have the strength. Despite what happened in the movies, no one really could pull themselves up by their fingertips. And then, most obvious of all, she didn't have the angle right. Every time she pushed off, she went out, not sideways. Not even King Kong had the reach to catch the roof with the way she was swinging.

What was it about rich people that made them completely ignorant of reality? Anybody with an ounce of real life experience would know this wasn't the way to roof a house. Or get back up on a house. But there she was swinging back and forth as if it made perfect sense. Of course, now that he looked at her, she didn't look like she was dripping in diamonds despite the fact that this was a ritzier area of Evanston. The only expensive thing she had on was that pretty pink bra with the torn piece of lace. He noticed because he couldn't help looking at the way the bit of fabric swung back and forth next to her cleavage. Meanwhile, he waited for her to realize her mistake, taking a step back to see if he could spot another way. That's when he chanced to look at the rope.

Oh shit, it was fraying.

The thin nylon cord was rubbing against the metal gutter as she swung. It couldn't hold out against her weight and the steady sawing motion.

"Stop!"

Too late. He heard it pop right when she was in full swing up toward the roof.

Just like catching a bad pass. He calculated the angle of her fall and leaped into position before she even recognized the problem.

Except she wasn't shaped anything like a basketball. And she didn't exactly fall neatly into his hands like one.

He didn't hear her scream, which he logged firmly in the plus column. He heard a gasp of surprise but nothing more. Then she landed in a diagonal sprawl of arms and legs that thunked into his chest like a pillowy train.

His shoulder screamed, but he'd braced enough to protect it from the worst of the impact. Normally, he could have held her aloft. Normally, his shoulder wouldn't be a lightning poker of fire because of his torn rotator cuff. But this wasn't a normal summer by any means, and so he couldn't fully support her weight.

Not a problem though because he'd stopped the momentum of her headfirst plummet. Even as his legs were bending to absorb most of her weight, he was able to maneuver her bottom half down. He heard the soft impact of her feet in the dirt, but supported every other part of her tight against his body. Hips, torso, those beautiful breasts— everything was pressed sweetly against his body.

Then it was over. Her feet were on the ground, her body was clasped tight in his good arm, and her face was pressed to his neck, her breath quick and hot against his skin. He breathed a sigh of relief and started to adjust her body against him. That was his mistake.

Pain seared up his neck and into his brain. Ice pick type of pain, and—fuck—he knew what that meant. He'd just made his rotator worse. His potentially career-ending injury was now worse. Jesus, the pain was throbbing through his brain. He let go with his right hand, doing everything he could to save his shoulder. She was on her feet at least so she didn't stumble, but she was still flopped awkwardly against his chest.

"Did we land in the flox? I can't see."

Flox? He didn't even know what flox was. "Straighten up," he growled. He couldn't take care of his shoulder if she didn't get off him. Fuck, it hurt. But even worse was the knowledge that he'd just delayed his recovery by God-only-knew how long.

"They're probably doomed," she said with a sigh, her breath feathering across his chest as she tried to extricate herself from his hold. But her legs got tangled in his, and her arms were awkwardly placed with her left one beneath one shoulder, and the right one over the other.

"I landed there on Monday while trying to clean out the gutters."

Jesus. If she would just freaking support her own weight he could deal with his pain. She managed it finally, but only after jarring his shoulder again. A list of profanities blew through his mind, and a few spilled out of his mouth behind his clenched jaw. Distantly he heard her squeak in alarm, but that was it. A tiny mouse sound amid the storm of agony in his shoulder.

He focused on that sound. It was high and came from somewhere near his left ear. And then he felt her hands on his face. Soft. Gentle. A stroke across his jaw in a steady, sweet rhythm.

He concentrated on that, letting it consume his whole attention while his breath eased, the pain dulled and he could slowly, inevitably open his eyes.

The first thing he saw was her clear blue eyes, wide and worried. The next was the sweet red bow of her lips. She had a peaches and cream complexion that was rosy in just the right places.

Beautiful.

Then she shook her head. "You should have told me you were hurt. We could have thought of a different way for me to fall. On a mattress or something."

Too bad she was a complete ditz.

Chapter Two

He gave her a tolerant smile. The one reserved for lunatics and the terminally ill. But since that proved he wasn't dying, Tori exhaled in relief. She could tell the strain around his eyes and mouth had eased with just that small gesture. If she could make him laugh, then everything would be okay. Or at least less bad. And lucky for him, she could make just about anyone laugh. Usually at her, but at the moment, she would make the sacrifice.

She looked down at the ground and huffed out an annoyed breath at the small patch of now trampled greenery. "We've killed it for sure."

He sighed, sounding very much like Edward at his most impatient. It was not an endearing sound. "What have we killed?"

"My flox," she said. "It's not your fault."

"I was saving your life—"

"I know. Thank you. I think they were doomed anyway from the other day."

He'd immobilized his arm against his chest. She tried not

to notice how broad his chest was but he was so tall that his torso filled practically her entire field of view. "You fell off the roof before?" he asked, clearly doubting her sanity.

"No. Off a tall chair. That's when I thought to get up on the roof." She frowned at him. "Shouldn't we be putting ice on that or something?" She gestured to her house. "I've got ice inside—"

He shook his head. "I've got it at my place."

He nodded and turned toward the street while she kept pace with him. He wasn't laughing yet, and as he had saved her life, she intended to do what she could for him. "I think I'll put in a rock garden," she said. "Instead of the flox."

"Then you'd be falling on rocks instead of trampled greenery. Or me." He frowned at her. "Don't you want to get dressed?"

She belatedly realized she was walking beside him topless except for her favorite bra. "Damn," she murmured as she fussed with the dangling lace. "I must have torn this when I dove after the roofing tiles."

"You—" He cut off his breath. "I don't want to know."

She stared at him, a little amused that this big hottie of a guy was clearly embarrassed by her undressed state. He was carefully looking everywhere but at her chest. "This is a full coverage bra. Swimsuits are more revealing than this. Not to mention bikinis or the average sports bra."

"This is a suburban neighborhood. With kids."

"It's a swim top," she lied. "And you're being ridiculous."

He huffed out a breath as they rounded the hedge. "You're the one talking about flox and a rock garden."

She was failing at making him laugh. Damn it, she had to distract him from his pain and if that meant parading around in her bra and speaking nonsense, then she'd do it. "Sure, make fun. But rock gardens are sacred to many religions including the Hindu and Buddhist."

He was moving gingerly, his fingers easily managing her fence latch even though she could never do it without both hands. "Are you Hindu or Buddhist?" he asked.

Her religious affiliation was a complicated matter, though of course, she was a student of all of them. "I kill plants."

"Wouldn't that make you a Satanist?"

She knew he was teasing her, but she found people laughed more if she pretended not to understand their jokes. "Oh no. More Wiccen, I believe. They sacrifice plants in most of their rituals. The Satanists are more into bloodletting." She peered more closely at his shoulder. "You're not bleeding are you?"

"Not externally."

Which suggested he had internal bleeding. Oh shit. She started searching for her cell phone to call 911, but it was still up on the roof.

"Damn it," she muttered as she about-faced.

"Where are you going?"

"If you're bleeding internally, you need to lie down. Stay calm. I'm getting my phone off the roof." She stopped long enough to grab her tee off the ground and throw it at him. It wasn't much, but basic first aid taught that shock victims need to stay warm. "And put that on."

"What? Wait!"

He was getting more excited and that was bad. Even worse he was moving to follow her. She whipped around and used her best teacher voice. "I told you to lie down, sir, and I mean it!"

He gaped at her. "Did you just go mama bear on me?"

She blinked. "Teacher bear."

He chuckled. At last! "I'm not dying," he said.

"You said you had internal injuries."

"Bruising is an internal injury."

Oh. Right. Then before she could say more, he held up his

good hand.

"I just need ice. And my painkillers."

"I will help you to your home."

"I can walk just fine." Then he threw her tee at her face and it landed with a soft *whump*.

She lifted her chin even though it was now buried beneath cotton fabric. "I'm helping you anyway," she said. When she pulled the tee away, he was glaring at her, clearly disgruntled. That was not what she wanted, so she decided to give him a gift. She pulled on her tee with rapid jerks. "There you go. No longer are you tempted to look down and scar your vision with my voluptuous mammary glands."

She thought he would scowl at her. Edward would always say something caustic when she got sarcastic. But just as she was bracing to be insulted, he started to laugh. It was a low rumble that began as a chuckle but kept going until she had to call it a laugh. It was a lovely sound. Deep and manly. It stirred happy memories of her father reading something especially delightful. In truth, it made her want other things too that had nothing to do with her parent. But that might be a function of him being a large, handsome man with the body of an Adonis.

"Where do you live?" she asked.

He jerked his chin to the house right on the other side of her fence. "Next door." He used his free hand to wrap around his chest, apparently trying to reach the right side pocket in his shorts. He didn't bother stifling his curse this time. "Can you grab the key out of my pocket?"

She folded her arms across her chest, as much to fight the urge to dig around very intimately in his pockets. "The Ketchums live there. She makes the best pies and he's a retired school teacher."

"And they're away on a two-month cruise courtesy of their son." He waited a moment for some reason, his gaze both wary and expectant. But she didn't know anything about the Ketchums' son and so she said nothing. Then he sighed for some mysterious reason. "I'm house-sitting."

She thought about that for a moment. In her experience house sitters were college kids who needed a cheap place to live for the summer, but that might just be because her entire life revolved around a college campus. Who was she to wonder if the Ketchums picked a modern-day Hercules to watch their house?

She might have questioned him further. He just didn't fit as a house sitter. He was too big and confident. Not that house sitters couldn't have their act together, but as a general rule, they didn't. Not if they were still doing odd jobs at his age which had to be in his early thirties.

But since he'd just saved her life and was looking more strained by the second, she decided to give him the benefit of the doubt. So she gestured for him to precede her to the Ketchums' house.

He all but rolled his eyes at her. What? Couldn't a woman be skeptical? Apparently not. But he resolutely crossed to his front door, then raised his eyebrows at her. "Now's where you get that key. It's in my shorts. Right side." He angled his hips and even pulled up his hoodie enough to show her the cut beauty of his physique.

She had to admit she was impressed. Michelangelo had sculpted bodies like this. Pristine marble that demonstrated a thorough understanding of anatomy. But this man was alive, his flesh rippling as he moved.

Her fingers itched to stroke that skin, so she folded her arms tight to her body. "You are fully capable of getting that key."

He looked at her, his jaw tightening. "I don't need to resort to cheap tricks to get fondled by a woman. My arm's immobilized, I'm going to call my doctor the moment I get inside, and damn it...will you please just get my fucking keys?"

Okay. So her attempt at humor hadn't worked. And perhaps he was in a lot more pain than she realized. So with a quick nod, she reached forward and pulled out the key ring. It was a quick movement, done in the blink of an eye. Or so she pretended.

Actually, her hand had to flatten across his hip to grab it. Heat and iron muscles rippled underneath her palm. The thin nylon of his shorts did nothing to blunt the cut tightness of his body. Wow. Had the temperature just shot up twenty degrees? And then the answer clicked in her mind.

"Are you a cover model?" That would explain why he was house-sitting. From what she understood, they weren't paid a lot.

"I'm an athlete." He ground out the words as he snatched the keys out of her hand. "Pro." That last word was punctuated with a glare.

Touchy touchy. Or perhaps—she grudgingly admitted—in a lot of pain. She stood back, watching him unlock the front door while she searched her memory. She didn't follow sports at all, but she had lived in Chicago for the last four years. Some sports were hard to miss even when one lived in an ivory tower, and that included basketball. Granted, this man didn't play for the Chicago Bulls, but he was a thorn in their side, or so her fellow professors claimed. And now that she'd placed him, she wanted to whack herself in the head for her stupidity. In her defense, he'd grown out his hair, hiding the signature eagle tattoo. Plus no one expected the famous Knicks point guard Michael Giamaria to be house-sitting next door.

So, a NY Knickerbocker was house-sitting in Chicago. No one would believe her if she told them that. And worse, what the hell did she say to him now?

While she pondered her next attempt to get him to laugh,

he opened the door and pushed into the modest ranch-style home. He didn't even glance back at her as she trailed in behind.

"I've got it," he grumbled. "You can go home now." Then a pause before his tone moderated a tad. A very tiny tad. "Thanks."

"I can help with the ice," she said, loath to leave him alone. He was injured from rescuing her. The least she could do was help with the ice. And if he had to take off his shirt to do it, so much the better.

He didn't respond, but walked deeper into the house. She looked around as she followed, appreciating the simple decor. Her aunt's house was cluttered with knickknacks of every sort on top of fussy Laura Ashley prints. This house had simple brown paneling, beige carpet, and nicely polished wood furniture. Very serviceable and very clean.

But then she stepped into the kitchen/family room combination. Clearly this is where the Ketchums lived. The large kitchen was very modern. Had to be, she supposed, to accommodate a prize-winning pie maker. And it attached onto a family room dominated by a very large, very big screen TV.

It was also, she noted, where her neighbor spent his time. She saw free weight equipment scattered over the room, plus various other electronics. A quick perusal showed her an e-reader and iPad on the coffee table, plus a laptop on the counter that faced the television. That's where her neighbor went—the counter—except he reached behind the laptop to pull out a medicine bottle. He tried to open the childproof cap one-handed, but this proved too much for his big hands.

"I got it," she said, coming closer. She took the bottle from his hands, feeling the warmth of his fingers entwining with hers for a brief moment. Damn, she'd always been a sucker for a guy's hands. Large, strong, and full of power. His were at least a size larger than she'd thought possible on a man, and she couldn't stop the tease of arousal that whispered through her body.

She stepped away, opening the cap. "How many do you need?" she asked, but he was already there taking the medicine from her hand.

One-handed, he tapped out two pills onto the counter, then he quickly threw them back, swallowing them dry.

"I always choke when I do that," she said, watching the way his Adam's apple bobbed. Even his neck was muscular, she realized.

He didn't respond. Instead, he thumbed on the iPhone on the counter, punching the second speed dial before putting it to his ear. Well, if he was going to ignore her, the least she could do is try to be useful. She'd get him ice, but first she needed a baggie to put it in. So she started pulling open drawers.

He spun around and frowned at her. "What are you doing?"

"Looking—"

"Hey Joey," he interrupted, speaking into the phone. "Call me. I…" He sighed, and there was a wealth of frustration in the sound. "I think I messed up."

He meant *she* messed up by falling onto him. Crap, she was just now processing that she'd seriously hurt him. Sure, she knew he'd wrenched something, but damaging an accountant's shoulder wasn't that big a deal. Or a car salesman or an electrician. Any of a zillion other jobs. But he was a pro athlete. And not just any pro but a multi-million-dollar megastar.

Damn. But at least she'd found the baggies. She pulled out the box with a ta-da motion only to have him thumb his phone off, stomp to the freezer and grab a cold pack off a shelf. No baggie required.

Oh.

He slapped it too hard onto his chest, the super-sized blue Ace pack whipping over his shoulder to slap against this back. Of course the hoodie kinda dulled the impact. And the cooling effect.

"That would probably be more effective without the sweatshirt."

"I know," he said, his words clipped. But of course, she saw the problem even before he tried to haul off his sweatshirt one-handed. Not going to be easy to take off his shirt while keeping the shoulder immobilized.

"Let me help," she said.

He glanced at her, and she could see he wanted to refuse. He was getting surlier by the second, and she was struggling to think of ways to make him laugh. In fact, this was starting to feel eerily like the last few years with Edward, and she'd just made a big and clear break from the let-me-tease-you-into-a-good-mood lifestyle. So instead of cracking a joke, she simply stood there and waited for him to either throw her out or acknowledge that he needed some help.

It took about twenty more seconds of him fumbling one-handed, but in the end, he huffed out a breath. "If you could…"

"Of course," she said sweetly. "I'd be happy to help, Mr. Tiger…er, Mr. Woods." She knew he wasn't Tiger Woods, but a horrible part of her personality couldn't help but poke at inflated egos. And superstar athletes were the worst of the bunch. Not that she knew any, but still.

It took him a moment to realize what she'd said. Long enough for her to have buried him in the depths of his hoodie such that his sputtering was muffled by the fabric. Or maybe he was cursing because she couldn't help but jostle his arm.

Shit.

But then he emerged, and his eyes were flashing fire. "Golf? Seriously?"

She put on her most clueless blonde look and blinked at

him. Then she grabbed the ice pack and pressed it—gently—to his shoulder. Or rather it would have been gently if he hadn't been moving to do the same thing. As it was, the impact was a little bit harder than she intended.

He hissed slightly in reaction, and she settled the rest of the long blue pack over his back. The thing was cold enough to bother her fingers, but he made no more response as she settled it tight against his body.

Well. Taut male physique exposed here for her perusal. She couldn't fault the view, that was for sure. She wondered just what the average basketball bunny would give to be where Tori was standing right now: in front of a wounded and mostly naked Michael Giamaria.

Meanwhile, Mr. Superstar Athlete was still annoyed she hadn't recognized him. "I'm not Tiger Woods," he groused.

"Really?" she said in her most innocent voice.

He studied her, then a moment later cursed under his breath. "You're teasing me. You know who I am."

"Does it matter?" she challenged. If he expected her to ask for his autograph, he was sadly mistaken. "I'm Tori Williams, by the way."

"Hello Tori," he said, but his tone was still miffed. He leaned over in his chair, far enough to reach a pile of brown Ace bandages stacked neatly in the corner. He grabbed three—his hand was that large—then started to unravel one before pressing the end to the front of the ice pack. "Hold it here?"

It was a question, but she bristled at his order. It wasn't rational. Edward had done that a million times to her. Phrasing an order as a question. So because she knew that she was reacting irrationally, she held one end of the bandage down then wrapped it as he directed.

Just as she was halfway through the third Ace, his phone rang. He thumbed it on with his good hand and pressed it to his ear.

"Joey?"

She was so close she could hear the other end of the conversation clear as a bell. "What the fuck did you do?"

"Caught an acrobat out of the air." He glanced up at her when he said it and if she were in a more charitable mood, she might have smiled. Instead, she felt a wave of guilt. What if she'd just ended his career?

"What?" Joey asked on the other end. Well, that and a string of profanity. Tori distracted herself from her guilt by appreciating the rhythm of the curses. It was almost iambic pentameter.

Meanwhile, Michael was grimacing into the phone. "Stop it, Joey. Look, can you come check it out? Or Doc? And bring the Cortisone."

"Doc's already on his way. I'd come over, too, if this traffic would fu—"

Michael thumbed off the phone mid-curse, but he didn't look up. His gaze was on the phone and his thoughts a million miles away. Probably on the problems his one Good Samaritan moment had caused in his life. She silently sent up a prayer to the Unifying Force of All Good that the damage was minor. She'd never forgive herself if her stupidity on the roof had ended his career.

In the end, she cleared her throat and stepped away. "So your friend's on his way over—"

"Doc. And yeah."

"Do you need me to wait around?"

"And trade golf tips?"

Was that a joke? Probably, but she was feeling too guilty to react appropriately. So she flashed him her most idiot blonde smile and waved at her house. "I'll just go back to my roofing—"

"No!"

She swallowed. Okay. Well, she was feeling a little hot anyway. "Um, okay. Rock garden it is. But, you know, if you need anything else, I'm right next door."

"I need you to stay off that roof." Then he rubbed his face. "Look, just get a thicker rope, okay? At least tie yourself off with the right type of rope."

She nodded. Good advice. She could get it at the rock store. Er, garden store. "Okay, then…" She'd already been backing away so it was an easy thing to give him a last wave and let herself out.

Once outside in the sunshine, she took a deep breath and closed her eyes. Well, this was a day for her diary. The day she'd ended the career of one of the country's favorite sons. She sighed as she started walking away. Normally, she'd be thinking of ways to make it up to the man, but honestly, she already knew that wouldn't be possible. First off, there wasn't anything anyone could do to make up for that type of disaster. Second, they were completely incompatible as friends. Or even friendly neighbors.

She resented anyone who thought he could order her not to roof her own house. And he was too much mega ego sports jock for her to find anything but his physique appealing over the long haul. In short, it would be best if she just let him be. After all, even in Evanston, neighbors didn't have to be friendly.

Decision made: she'd ignore him. And with that thought in mind, she headed off to the garden store to buy some decorative rocks.

Chapter Three

"What part of 'rest and recovery' didn't you understand?"

Mike grimaced at Doc and just shook his head. "She fell off her roof. Was I supposed to just let her die?"

For a middle-aged white guy with a paunch, Doc had a glare that could make even him squirm. But he didn't break. He would not feel bad about saving Tori's life. So, eventually, the man grunted and returned to pushing annoying fingers into his painful shoulder.

"You sure she fell by accident?"

"You're kidding, right?" Mike's gaze cut to a man he trusted with his life. He was damned lucky that the guy had decided to spend the summer with his daughter in Chicago. That meant the man was on call night and day to save Mike's bacon—or shoulder—as it were. That and Joey, personal trainer to the megastars, and he was set for Evanston rest and rehab. "She fell off her roof."

"Women have done crazier things to get into your bed."

"They have not. She fell off—"

"Her roof. Yeah, I heard that."

Mike sighed. "Look, it's different out here. She didn't recognize me."

Doc grunted as he raised Mike's arm slowly, watching for the moment Mike grimaced. "Out here? You mean in far-off Evanston?" The man rolled his eyes. "They have TVs here too. Big screen monstrosities. Bulls Fever hits here just like the rest of Chicago. And everybody knows the point guard who fed the Bulls their lunch."

"That doesn't even make sense." Mike winced as Doc shifted his arm too quickly. "She thought I was Tiger Woods."

"Bullshit."

Mike nodded, still feeling the prick to his ego at the idea. "She might have been joking," he grudgingly admitted.

Doc snorted. "You megastars. If it's not the booze and other shit—"

"I don't do that," he snapped. Outside of the obvious reason that his body was his career and he didn't screw with his career, his mother would kill him if she found out. The one time he'd come home drunk, she'd tanned his hide so hard he couldn't sit for a week.

But Doc was unimpressed. "If it's not that shit, then it's the women."

Mike felt his jaw clench. "I don't do the women either. You know that."

"Not during the season. You're on rest and recovery vacation now."

Mike opened his mouth to argue, but then had to bite back a groan as Doc moved his arm in a particularly painful way.

"And you do do the women," the man continued. "Lots of them. Just not before a game."

Mike wanted to jerk his arm back and away from the sadistic doctor, but he knew better. So he sat there and groused. "Those aren't women. Not like you mean. They're just—"

"Basketball bunnies are women too. They're just easy women."

Easily had, easily forgotten. That was different. Tori was different. She came off as a total ditz, but there had been something in her expression that belied that impression. As if she was purposely pretending to be clueless. He had no idea how much was true, and how much was an act.

Meanwhile, Doc finished with his shoulder—thank God—then he rocked back on his heels. Mike waited while the bastard stared at him with that blank-faced silent shit that never failed to make Mike nuts.

"What?"

"The burbs don't agree with you. Why don't you go back to New York?"

"I hate that circus. And I'm kinda getting fond of sidewalk chalk."

"And women that fall from the sky?"

Mike crossed his arms—gingerly. "She could have died."

"Just don't screw your career."

And right there was the crux of the problem. "How bad is it?"

Doc huffed out a breath while Mike held his. "You've put yourself back a month at least, so the pre-season's out."

Yeah, he'd already guessed that.

"But if you do everything exactly as I tell you, then I think you'll be okay for the regular season."

"Yes!"

"But don't fuck up. And don't—"

"Fuck her. Yeah, I got it."

Doc frowned. "I was going to say don't fuck with your system. It got you to being a Knicks superstar. Don't abandon it now."

"That's the same thing." His system was really simple.

Anything that interfered with his game was avoided like the plague. Booze harder than beer and any recreational drugs were the easiest of the distractions to avoid. Gambling was his father's sin, so Mike didn't even play Lotto. Naw, his problem had always been the girls. Serious girls seriously screwed up his game. So if he couldn't bed 'em and forget 'em, then he avoided them. "And for the record, I don't even like her. She's a rich white girl who hasn't got the brains God gave a gnat. And she knows shit about basketball. Or golf."

Doc didn't comment as he lifted up Mike's bottle of prescription painkillers. Then he turned and dropped them in his bag. "I'm taking these."

"What? Why?" He had a pretty high tolerance for pain, but sometimes his shoulder ached so bad he couldn't sleep.

"So you remember to protect it. And stop thinking you're Superman rescuing damsels in distress."

"Jesus, Doc, I saved her life."

"And now you can suffer the consequences." The man pulled out a pad and started scribbling, but that didn't stop him from talking. "A few beers are fine, but be careful of the calories. The key is moderation which I know is a hard concept for you athletes to understand." And that was that. Well, that was all the chitchat. The rest was the serious business of rehab schedules, crazy-making exercises three times a day. "Not seven, not ten," the doc stressed. "And certainly not forever. Just three. Slowly. And you stop if there's pain."

"There's always pain."

"Suck it up." Doc's last words before he left. In fact, those were always his last words.

And Mike listened.

Mike was finishing off his turkey burger when he heard the

commotion. He was on his back deck, enjoying the beautiful evening and listening to the Tigers play baseball. He might live in New York—and temporarily in Chicago—but he'd been born and raised in Detroit. He was a Tiger baseball fan and would be until the day he died.

So he'd turned on the game through his iPhone, settled on the back deck with lemon water—it didn't have enough sugar to be called lemonade—and …well, and he waited to see if his neighbor decided to try and kill herself again by roofing.

She hadn't, as far as he was aware. She'd spent the rest of yesterday and most of today on her new rock garden. She'd switched off of whatever drum beat thing she'd been listening to on the roof to the Beatles. He'd heard just enough of *Ticket to Ride*—sung in a sweet alto—to settle into memories of his grandmother and chocolate chip cookies.

A perfect night until a car pulled into her driveway and a man pounded on Tori's door.

"Tori! Tori!" There was definite fury in the man's voice, but Mike recognized an undercurrent of panic as well. The guy left off pounding on the door to rush around her house. He cursed as he tripped over the roofing tiles on the ground, then cursed again as he ran foul of the rock garden. Mike had a perfect view because he'd stood up to see over the fence.

The starting-to-bald thin guy in khaki pants and a polo had made it up to Tori's back door and was pounding on it now, his curses taking on a more vehement edge.

Mike left his deck to head around the hedge. The guy was making enough noise to alert the entire neighborhood. If Tori didn't respond to that, then something really could be wrong.

He was just rounding the edge of the fence when he heard the back door wrench open.

"Shit, Edward, you scared me half to death."

"Me?" the guy squeaked. "Damn it, Tori, I've been calling you for hours. What the hell? Are you all right?"

"Of course I'm all right. I've been making pies."

"Pies? I've been worried sick. Why didn't you answer your phone?"

Even from across the backyard, Mike could hear the woman huff in disgust. "Because it's not going to rain for another couple days."

Edward was understandably confused by this statement, but Mike had spent enough time in Tori's company to get an idea of her thought process. Unlike the pompous Edward, Mike knew that her phone was still up on the roof. Apparently, Tori had decided to leave it up there. There was no danger because it wasn't going to rain.

"Tori, you're not making any sense," Edward said, each word pronounced with sharp derision.

"Yes, I am," she returned hotly. "Besides, no one important was going to call me anyway."

"I was calling!"

Tori didn't answer; her silence a clear slap on the guy's face. Mike had to stifle his laugh. Meanwhile, Edward shifted his tactics, his tone becoming both wounded and condescending at the same time.

"That's not fair, Tori. You know I worry about you. We all do. You're not used to living alone. And this house—"

"Oh hi, Mike," Tori interrupted. "Come on in. I've been making pies for you."

Mike should have felt guilty for eavesdropping, but he didn't. Not with the offer of pie. So he grinned and sauntered forward. Doc's words about not fucking Tori wandered through his mind, but he escorted the words right back out. He wasn't going to screw Tori. He was going to enjoy some pie.

Meanwhile, Edward turned around, his eyes widening when he saw him. Then Mike waited, expecting the usual frown before shocked recognition.

He waited. And waited.

"I thought you said an old couple lived next door," Edward said, his voice and attitude wary.

"Mike's house-sitting. And encouraging me to make a rock garden." She gestured to the side of her yard where a seemingly haphazard collection of rocks clustered. One boulder, painted hot pink, stood regally over five medium rocks, each a different neon color, near a collection of smaller stones of natural color laid in a circle.

"Very nice," Mike said because that's what a man says when offered free pie.

"Is that what I tripped over? Good God, Tori, I thought it was debris from the roof."

"It's a work in progress," she said stiffly. "Come on in, Mike. The pies are almost done."

Now that he was closer, he could smell them. Hot pie, fresh from the oven. He was already salivating and a quick mental calculation told him he could afford the calories if he cut back tomorrow and ran a few extra miles.

"Tori!" Edward exclaimed, but she had already given the man her back.

Mike didn't bother to hide his grin as he pushed his way through the back door. He was about to head for the kitchen by smell alone but he had to stop to look at her family room. Or should he say disaster zone?

The furniture was scattered—or stacked—mostly in the corner. She'd ripped up the carpet, so he stepped onto the unfinished wood underneath. To one side was a stack of books, spilling out of three moving boxes. To the other side was a kitchen filled with knickknack chickens of every size and ilk. The largest one was a concrete rooster, frozen in the act of cock-a-doodle-doing. The smallest were the zillions of chickens scattered about the wallpaper. The others were just too many to take in, including seven sets of chicken salt and pepper shakers all lined up along the counter wall.

"Chicken pot pie, anyone?" he quipped as he stepped in.

Tori laughed. Or rather she started to, but then tried to stifle it. So it came out as more of a snort that he found charming anyway.

"I was going to rip down the wallpaper, but then I noticed that my cooking splatters were kind of like food for the chickens. So I've decided to leave it for now."

"Good idea," he said with a chuckle.

Then Edward trailed in. "This place is a death trap. What happens if you start sleepwalking again? God only knows what will happen."

"I expect I'll trip over something and wake up." She leaned down to pull the pies out from the oven, treating Mike to a nice view of her backside. She was wearing cutoffs again which hugged her ass perfectly. Not to mention the length of creamy thigh underneath.

Next to him, Edward sighed in frustration. "Tori…" he said. Mike didn't know whether it was in annoyance about her lack of sleepwalking precautions or because those shorts were just shy of indecent. Either way, the man was becoming a first-class bore.

But before he put the prick in his place, Mike needed to understand the relationship. Edward spoke to Tori like an irritated older brother, but there was no family resemblance between them. She was a slender blonde with crystal clear blue eyes and legs that went on for miles even on her petite frame. Edward, on the other hand, was a dumpy looking white guy with curly brown hair and horn-rimmed glasses over mud-colored eyes.

Meanwhile, Tori had just set two lumpy looking pies on the stove. One of them had clearly spilled over, its reddish brown innards burned onto the cookie tray. Once those were set down, she pulled off her rooster-shaped oven mitts and turned to face Edward.

"If I promise to answer the phone, will you leave?"

"Only if I can see that it's charged." He looked over at Mike. "I can't tell you how many times I've tried to call her only to find her dead phone sitting beside our bed. Or lost under it."

Uh-oh. *Our* bed didn't sound like something a brother would say.

Tori sighed and stepped around them, heading for the back door. "Fine. I'll get it."

Mike was still trying to picture Tori sleeping with this jerk when he suddenly realized what she intended to do. He was out of his chair and rushing after her a second later. "Don't—" he began, but it was too late.

She was already climbing the tree, her blond hair was so white it seemed spooky in the fading light.

"What's she doing?" Edward called from still inside the house. Mike looked back to see him turning off the oven.

"Getting her phone," Mike answered, trying to keep his voice calm. It was twilight. She hadn't taken a flashlight of any kind. If she took a misstep, no way would Mike be able to catch her again. He could move his shoulder without much pain—thanks to the anti-inflammatories—but his arm didn't have any strength. A little bit of strain and the whole thing just quit working.

He stepped out into her backyard, choking back his words. He wanted to tell her to be careful, but he remembered his daredevil niece. The moment someone said "be careful" was the exact second the child would make a show of exactly how daring she was. Tori wasn't that childish, but she certainly wouldn't appreciate him hovering either. So he held his tongue and didn't clue Edward in on the possible disaster-to-be.

Then he heard the shadow of her body speak. "Call my phone, will you?"

Hell. She couldn't find it. He fished his phone out of his pocket. "What's your number?"

She recited it, and he dialed. A second later a man's voice pealed out. "Tori, pick up the phone. Tori, stop reading. Pick up the phone."

Then it stopped, and he heard her voice through his cell saying, "Found it."

"Is that your ringtone?" he asked.

"I know. Obnoxious, but Edward thought it was funny. Come to think of it…"

She suddenly hung up. He waited, peering into the darkness and trying to pick out her silhouette. Then tiny electronic notes sounded. Then piano chords. Next came a train whistle.

It took him a moment to understand that she was changing her ringtone right there on the roof. He grinned. Of course she would change it right then and there. She was an immediate-thought kind of girl.

"Take your time," he said. "Figure it out before you start back."

He heard a dull thump as she settled down on the roof. "It's a nice night. Tell me when he's gone."

Trumpets blared. Another ringtone choice.

"You've got my number," he said. "Call me when you're ready to come down. I'll spot you, just in case."

A cascade of electronic notes came next.

"I'm not going to rip up your shoulder twice in one week."

"Just in case, Tori. Okay?"

"Sure."

The *Twilight Zone* music sounded.

He waited a moment more, but she seemed well occupied. He turned back to the door only to see Edward heading out of it.

"What is she doing?" the man demanded.

"Changing her ringtone."

The man rolled his eyes. Jesus, he'd never seen a grown adult do that before. "Typical. Just typical," Edward groused.

"If you don't mind my asking, exactly what is your relationship with Tori?"

Edward headed back inside, aiming straight for her refrigerator. "I'm her fiancé, that's what. Or I will be as soon as she gets this silliness out of her system." He waved over his shoulder at the house in general.

Popping open the refrigerator, the man searched for something, then grumbled when he didn't find it. He straightened up with another roll of his eyes. "Yogurt, brussels sprouts, and peanut butter." He pulled out the jar of Jiff from the back of the appliance. "She doesn't even know that this gets hard when it's cold."

He slammed it down on the counter and looked at Mike who had no answer. Sure, he liked room temperature peanut butter as much as anyone, but he got the feeling the man's fury wasn't because the condiment was cold.

"So, you're engaged?"

Edward leaned back against the counter. "No. Yes. Well, no."

"She either said yes or she didn't."

He sighed. "Actually, it's more like I haven't asked yet. Then she got mad about some stupid sushi book and stormed over here to renovate this disaster."

Mike looked around. It was clear that there were half-finished projects everywhere he looked. But it also seemed like she must have been here a while. After all, no one could partially start this many projects in a day or so.

"Exactly how long has she been here?"

"Long enough to nearly die a hundred times." Edward cocked his head. "She's on the roof right now, isn't she?"

No sense in lying. "Yeah."

"In the dark where one misstep could pitch her over the edge. And did you see this?" He held up a book on the counter. It was covered in fruit stains, but the title was clear. *Wiring a House. For Pros by Pros.*

Mike tried to keep an open mind. "Does she have an electrical background?"

"She's a religion and philosophy professor at Northwestern." Edward dropped his head back against the cabinet. "Don't get me wrong. The woman's brilliant. Spent a year hanging out with the Dalai Lama. She knows kabalistic symbols and Hindi mumbo jumbo like the back of her hand. If it's esoteric, she's an expert. But ask her to put together a bookcase, and you'll have nails sticking out of your carpet. On a practical, real world basis, she's a hazard."

Mike wanted to give Tori the benefit of the doubt. There wasn't a single part of Edward that he liked, but he had to admit the man had a point. She had fallen off her roof.

So rather than talk about Tori's potential mishaps, he turned the conversation back to Edward. "You don't sound like you really want to marry her."

"Of course I do," he huffed. "We've been together for nearly five years. You don't throw that away because she inherited a death trap of a house."

That wasn't at all what Mike meant, but he'd learned early not to mess around in other people's relationships. So he pushed away from the counter. "Look, I'll just—"

"Do you want to make some money?"

Mike tilted his head, wondering if he'd heard correctly. "What?"

"Here's the problem: she's got this independent streak. All she needs is some time by herself to realize that she needs me. But she can't get time alone if I keep coming around checking up on her."

"So don't come around."

"I'm terrified she's going to kill herself. Her whole family is." He abruptly pulled out his wallet and counted out five twenties. "But if she has someone looking out for her. A neighbor that she trusts… You know, someone who will call 911 if she accidentally impales herself or something."

Mike's tone was cold. "I don't need money to call 911."

Edward didn't seem at all embarrassed. "Of course not. You're a good neighbor. But she's also got the worst judgment when it comes to people, especially men."

No argument there. After all, Tori had apparently picked this dick for half a decade.

"I've known her since college. You wouldn't believe the losers she was attracted to."

Mike was not going to say a word. Not. A. Word.

"So a good neighbor would see if she picks up some guy. If someone starts hanging around." He set his business card down on top of the stack of twenties. It read *Prairie State College* on top of it.

"You want me to call you if she starts dating." Mike folded his arms across his chest.

"Well, yeah. Look, I'm just worried about her. If you could keep an eye on her so I don't have to? Just check on her every night. Make sure she hasn't electrocuted herself." He gestured at the book on wiring.

"I can do that," he said. After all, he'd been planning to do that anyway from the moment he'd first seen the book on wiring. Or maybe it was from before. When he'd seen those legs pushing off the gutter as she tried to swing herself back onto the roof. Not to mention that delightful pink bra. "But I don't need your money."

"Great," Edward said with a smile. "And call me if you see something worrisome." He grabbed his business card and flipped it over before scrawling a phone number on the back. "That's my cell number. Call anytime."

He pushed the money forward. Mike didn't move.

"Please, Mike, I'm desperate here."

One hundred dollars didn't constitute desperate in Mike's book, but he didn't quibble.

"My only other choice is to keep stopping by myself and she needs her space. Just long enough to realize that she can't make it on her own."

"She's an adult with a good job. Of course she can make it on her own."

Edward rolled his eyes. "You'll see. She hasn't got any sense. She'll tumble off the roof or something if someone isn't there to keep an eye out."

There was no way to argue that. Which again showed that the man had a point. "I'll call you right after I dial 911, but I'm not keeping track of her dates," he said, though he didn't touch the stack of bills.

Edward released a breath. "Thank you. Now what's your cell number so I can call you?"

Mike shook his head. "I don't give that out."

"You don't— But how else am I to call you?"

Mike smiled. "Trust me. I'll call you if she's headed for the ER."

Edward stared at him, trying to intimidate him which was laughable. The day some balding guy with no muscles and a flabby gut intimidated him was the day Mike would hang up his athletic shoes for good.

In the end, the man huffed out a breath. "Fine. But if I don't hear from you soon, I'll have to stop by again. And that just isn't a good idea."

Mike nodded. "You better go now. Otherwise Tori might realize you're hanging around to keep an eye on her."

Edward huffed. "She's probably searching Navaho creation myths or something. Totally forgotten about me by now." There was real hurt in his words, and Mike could tell this was a man who liked having a doting woman at his side. Which meant Tori was the worst choice in the world. However had they stayed together for five years?

"I'll keep an eye out for you," Mike said. "But you should go."

"Fine. Fine. Let me just say good-bye." He started for the back door, but Mike stopped him.

"I'll tell her. If you startle her up there, she'd probably fall off the roof."

Edward laughed and it wasn't a very nice sound. "Probably. Okay. I'm going."

"Bye."

Edward wanted to go out by the back door, but Mike stood in front of it like a brick wall. In the end, he cast a last disgusted look about the living room disaster and shook his head.

"I wouldn't eat that pie, if I were you. Last time she cooked, she gave me food poisoning. I nearly died."

Then he was gone out the front door. A few minutes later, Mike heard the bang of the car door and the roar of a moron with a muscle car. Which is when he was startled by a quiet voice behind him.

"He's right, you know. I'm a terrible cook. But I think he already had the flu, so I plead a 'maybe' on the food poisoning. And he was a long way from dying."

Mike whirled around to see her in the doorway looking equal parts embarrassed and annoyed. "How much did you hear?"

She shrugged. "I didn't have to hear anything to know what he said. I'm hopeless and he needs to look out for me."

"He intends to marry you."

She shook her head. "I'll believe that when he gets down on one knee. Until then…" She gestured to the pies. "Eat at your own risk."

"Tell you what," he said as he pointed to Edward's wad of bills. "If it's terrible, we'll go out for dessert."

"And if it's wonderful?"

"We'll go out for steak tomorrow."

She seemed to think about it for a moment, then grinned. "You can have the steak. I'm a pescetarian."

He blinked at her. "I'm a Sagittarius." Then while she laughed, he grabbed a set of plates decorated with fluffy yellow chicks and prepared to risk his life with pie.

Chapter Four

Her pies were just fine, Tori thought with flushed pleasure. Bury anything in enough ice cream and it will taste good, right? Mike ate two pieces and finished off her ice cream, so she decided she'd done fairly well in her first dessert attempt. And while he was polishing off the last bite, she dropped her chin on her hand and asked the question that had been burning in her brain for at least two minutes now.

"Why didn't you tell Edward you're an NBA star?" She gestured at the stack of bills. "A hundred is nothing to you."

"A hundred is never nothing," he said as he leaned back in his chair.

"You make his yearly salary in one game. And that's whether you play or not."

"How'd you find out?"

She arched a brow. "I might be clueless about sports, but I do know how to use the internet. And even if I hadn't recognized you, I saw your name on the pill bottle." She looked at his shoulder. "I saw the CSPAN report too." Even now she winced in memory of him getting his shoulder practically ripped out of its socket. YouTube had it in glorious slow motion. "It seemed…odd. You don't normally play like that."

"No kidding," he said. When she frowned at him, he did a one-shoulder shrug. "I was playing in a charity basketball tournament. Went up to stuff a jump shot. It was a stupid show-boating move. I telegraphed it because there were cameras there. Got to get the pretty shot, right?" He was clearly angry with himself.

She knew next to nothing about basketball. Truthfully, she was hopeless about all sports, but she nodded sympathetically. "Well, the cameras got a good picture."

"Of me getting stuffed." He looked at her a moment and again must have realized she had no idea what he was talking about. "I went up to shoot"—he used his good arm to mime throwing a basketball into the air—"but then the other guy slapped it away right at the worst possible moment." His arm and his elbow went back at an awkward angle. "SLAP tear. Tore the rotator cuff."

"And then I made it worse," she said, guilt making her especially solicitous as she offered him more pie.

"My fault." He waved aside another piece and she started covering the thing with plastic wrap. It was a simple domestic act, done a thousand times. But this time, she was super conscious of her every move. And of the man sitting across from her, clearly depressed.

"It was just a silly accident," she tried. "People get too competitive in sports games."

He snorted at that, then looked embarrassed as he wiped his mouth on a paper towel. She hadn't thought to buy paper napkins. "If I'd paid attention to the game, I would have seen him coming. But my eyes were on the cameras. A stupid rookie mistake."

She stepped out from behind the kitchen island to face

him directly. "It was just a game. Completely unimportant."

He stared at her in shock. "No game is unimportant," he said.

Oh. Right. He would feel that way even though the idea was nearly incomprehensible to her. Disease was important and affairs of state were important—not that she paid much attention to either. But a game where only money and pride were on the line? She didn't understand that. She did, however, know that entertainers were important and so she put him in the same category as she would put a great bard—someone who brought richness and joy to people's lives even if she didn't fully understand the way he did it.

So she just looked at him and shook her head. "I can't believe you're living in the Ketchums' house." That would be like waking up one day to learn that Shakespeare had moved in next door.

"I'm hiding out. Got tired of the paparazzi hanging around my building and badgering me about my recovery. So when Joey told me his parents were leaving for the summer, I offered to house-sit."

"You could recover in a luxury spa somewhere."

He actually shuddered at the idea. "I don't want yoga and mud baths."

"And no one expects you to be living in Evanston?"

"Seen any reporters out there?"

She shook her head. "But it's early days yet. You just moved in yesterday."

"Four days ago."

She frowned, trying to think back. It didn't work. Without the daily schedule of a teaching week, her life was a disorganized progress of days. She never kept track of time. She never had any appointments to track. Eventually it would be September, and she'd have to look at a calendar. But right now was summer. And renovation. And a celebrity basketball star next door.

She wasn't sure how she felt about that, so she allowed herself to get distracted and pointed at the family room floor. "Do you think I should use carpet? Wood flooring is so much easier to maintain."

"And ten times as expensive."

True. "I haven't learned how to lay carpet. Wood is easier. It just takes a hammer and some glue."

He chuckled. "Most people hire someone to install their carpet. And roof their homes."

"Not if they're going to flip the house for profit."

His gaze slid over the chicken wallpaper. "You're intending to flip this?"

She looked at him, a little startled. Usually when she said a general statement about anything—selling this house or studying native American pottery—people nodded and assumed that meant she was going to do exactly what she suggested. Not him. He actually asked the question, and she was both flattered and unnerved by his intelligence.

"I...um," she said, floundering. "Why do you ask?"

He looked around. "Because it was your aunt's place. Because you're putting in a rock garden which doesn't figure into a bottom line. And because you looked over my shoulder when you answered."

She jerked her gaze back to his. "What?"

"When you're being evasive, you look over my shoulder. Or if I'm looking right at you, your feet get restless." He arched a brow. "I'm paid very well to read body movements."

"I've never held a basketball in my life."

"Doesn't matter. All life's a game in one way or another."

She tilted her head, extremely self-conscious now about where her eyes were. "That's a profound statement."

He burst out laughing, the sound filling her kitchen. "It's a greeting card philosophy, but in this case it's true." Then his expression sobered. "So what are you going to do?"

She shrugged. "Put in a rock garden and finish the roof." She didn't want to think beyond that right now.

He grinned. "So show it to me."

"What?"

"Show me what you're doing to the house."

She looked around. Every project was half begun, and the rooms she hadn't touched yet were either filled with her aunt's clutter or her own boxes that she'd packed as quickly as possible when leaving Edward's condo. "I don't really know what I'm doing." Then she paused. She'd given him an opening a mile wide, but he wasn't saying anything. In fact, after a moment, he frowned at her.

"What?"

"Why don't you tell me what you think I should do?" she prompted. That way she could pretend she was listening and not have to do anything more. But he shook his head.

"How should I know? It's your house."

She stared at him for a long time, her mind whirling. He waited patiently, practically challenging her to…to…she didn't know what. But it made her uncomfortable in a good way. Like she was discovering something new, and that always excited her.

"I think I'm out of practice," she finally said.

"At what?"

"At this. At talking."

He drained his glass of water. "Next time, I'm bringing the beer," he said as he set it down.

She smiled, liking the idea of doing this again. But then he stood up, towering over her as he flashed a grin. White teeth, caramel skin, liquid brown eyes. When she'd looked at him before, she saw his size and his chiseled body. Sex in raw masculine power. But this time what she saw was friendliness. There was an underlying ease with her that again felt very odd.

"What are you going to do?" she abruptly blurted.

"What…now?"

She hadn't meant now. She'd meant in general. How was she supposed to classify him in her mind? Neighbor who stopped by once in a while for pie? Professional athlete who was going to bring a parade of bimbos and reporters past her door? Did he plan on having loud parties? Or was he going to kiss her when he brought that beer over?

The thoughts spun, chaotic and confusing. But she was used to the whirl in her mind, even if it involved inappropriate thoughts about kissing. So she just looked at him and waited to see what he would say.

Besides, he was pretty to look at, especially when he grinned.

"I'm going to go walk carefully through your backyard. There's a rock garden out there, you know."

She grinned. "I know."

"And I'm going to do something else too."

"What?"

"It's a surprise."

"I don't like surprises."

"Everybody likes good surprises."

"Not me." Mostly because she never reacted the way people wanted. She was supposed to be thrilled when Edward showed her his new car, but she thought the seats were uncomfortable and didn't like the noise of his exhaust. She was supposed to be happy when her sister had given her a makeover as a PhD present, but she'd hated the feel of stuff on her face and didn't like the curly hairdo.

He held up Edward's wad of bills. "One hundred bucks says you'll like it."

She folded her arms. "I really hate surprises."

"Then it'll be the easiest money you've ever made."

"No one ever wins when they bet against me," she said.

He arched a brow. "You do know that I'm a pro ball player. Millions of people bet on me every game."

"Chickens have been sacred animals dating back to the Kianian Period in Iran." Then she paused as he frowned at her. "I thought we were stating irrelevant facts."

Once again his laughter rumbled through her kitchen. She really liked that sound.

Then he stopped laughing, though his eyes still sparkled with humor. "So do we have a bet?"

"Easiest hundred I'll ever make."

"Done."

And then he kissed her.

He was a big man with big hands that moved very quickly. He cupped her face, waited through her start of surprise, then bent his head to hers all in the space of a second. Her lips were parted and he had no trouble taking control of her mouth. He nipped at the edges of her lips—setting them to tingling—before he thrust inside. Teasing darts of his tongue, in and out in quick motions. A blitzkrieg of invasions while she scrambled to process what he was doing.

She couldn't do it. She couldn't keep up, and in that moment, her mind completely surrendered. Her body had already waved the white flag. So she arched into him, her arms gripping his arms as she drew herself up against him. And everything changed.

His tongue did not withdraw now. He thrust inside her and touched every part of her mouth. She dueled with him, each dominating stroke of his tongue making her hotter than she ever thought possible.

One kiss, and she was on fire.

And then he lifted his head. Belatedly she realized she was up on her toes, one knee lifted against his thigh. Holy shit.

"Surprise," he said.

It took her a moment to process what he'd done. The kiss had been the surprise, and there was no way she could claim she hadn't liked it. She'd all but climbed his leg.

"Wait a minute…"

He stepped back from her, a huge grin on his face. "Easiest hundred I've ever made." And then he was gone, his laughter filling her backyard.

•••

Jesus, smart women were such a turn-on. He was used to basketball bimbos. Big boobs and basketball stats were the sum total of their assets. Sure, he'd fucked them with gleeful abandon back in his earlier days. But sometime in the last five years, he'd grown bored with that. Though he always had a boobette on his arm in public, he never took them to bed. Hell, most never even saw the inside of his condo.

But Tori was different. A blonde waif with no makeup, zero interest in sports, and absolutely no homemaking skills whatsoever. At least her cleavage was nice, but that pie had been barely edible. Thank God for ice cream or he'd never have been able to choke down the first slice. But she'd seemed so pleased with herself that he hadn't wanted to hurt her feelings. Besides, he could eat anything. So he had, while she'd watched him with a stunned kind of pleasure. She'd been so pretty there, her eyes sparkling with happiness, that he'd scooped up another slice.

God, he was a sap.

And then he'd gone and kissed her.

Damn that kiss had been hot. It was all he could do to pull himself away, but a healthy sense of self-preservation had kicked in before he'd stripped her naked and fucked her against her chicken wallpaper.

She was not a basketball bimbo. She was as far from a

fuck-me girl as it was possible to get. And the last thing he needed was a real woman screwing with his game.

Other men could handle a girlfriend and still play at the top of their abilities. Other guys managed a wife and kids even, but he wasn't wired that way. He'd learned that the hard way in high school and then again in college. The minute a real woman entered his life, his game went to hell. Always had, always would.

Given that he wasn't a young twenty-something anymore and he'd just had the shit torn out of his shoulder, the last thing he needed to do was find a real woman. Not a bimbo but a girl with crystal blue eyes, straight blond hair, and a PhD. Jesus, she'd even spent a year with the Dalai Lama. Everything about Tori screamed "marry me," and he wasn't going down that route until he was done with basketball.

Which meant he'd stopped that amazing kiss before he'd flipped her over his good shoulder and carried her to bed. And now he was going home with a boner so hard he was walking funny.

By the time he made it home—after tripping over the tool belt she'd left in the middle of her lawn—he'd decided he'd never bring those beers over to her house. She was a menace and not because she was a disaster at home improvement. He had just under three months to rehab his shoulder and get into playing shape for the season opener in September.

Tori was a distraction, and he knew exactly how to deal with those: ball drills, free weights, and cold showers. And no more kisses. Ever.

That worked for the first day. He'd injured his dominant shoulder which gave him the perfect reason to practice with his non-dominant hand. Sadly, that thought only worked in theory. There was no way he could shoot, dribble, or pass— even one-handed—without using his bad shoulder a little. It moved whenever he moved, even if his right side never touched the ball.

Which is why Joey told him to go the fuck home. He hadn't even realized the trainer was in the building, but the man walked onto the court, grabbed the ball, and spoke his mind. Complete with about seven curses per sentence.

Day two was spent studying game footage and secretly listening for sounds of Tori up on her roof again. She didn't go there until late afternoon and he spent a miserable couple hours surfing the internet while surreptitiously watching to see if she took a header. He'd made sure she got the right kind of rope and was tied off properly, so she wasn't going to die, but the whole thing still gave him a headache.

Which is why he called his uncle in the roofing business. That was the other draw to Chicago: he had family living here. By the next morning, he was up on her roof—via a real ladder—and using his good arm in ways that it hadn't moved since high school. And yet it gave him great satisfaction to hammer nails while picturing Tori's face when she saw what he had done. He could just see her beaming smile.

About an hour into his work, he heard a car door slam. He was at an angle on the roof that he could see down into her driveway where Tori stepped out looking not at all like the Tori he'd met a few days ago.

She was in heels and a sundress that showed off her tanned legs to perfection. Her blond hair fell in soft waves about her shoulders, and her face—when she looked up to see him—had makeup that made her eyes huge, and the sunshine gave them a glow-like blue fire. He'd known that she was a beauty, but right then she was dressed to impress. And he was. So much so that he barely noticed the other woman getting out of the rental car beside her.

Then he grinned because Tori didn't go inside but headed around the house to the backyard. He moved quickly around the roof, aiming for the ladder, way too excited to see her appreciate his work. It was roofing, for God's sake. But he'd stayed away for almost three days and he was really looking forward to talking to her again.

But she didn't climb up the ladder. It took him a moment to realize she'd kicked off her sandals and was climbing up the tree.

"You know, there's a ladder right here…" he began, but then he took a look at her face. Oops. That was not the happy expression he was expecting but a pissed off woman face. "Um, Tori—"

"What the hell are you doing?"

Shit. Conversational minefield, but there was no way he couldn't answer. "Roofing."

"My house. My job. I don't need your big manly hands fixing my problems, thank you very much."

He kept his voice level, but that didn't stop the burn of anger in his gut. "I wasn't fixing your problems—obviously. I was working on your roof."

"I didn't ask you to."

"I was being helpful."

"I just want people to leave me the fuck alone!" She stomped over to his ladder and shoved it off so that it landed with a clatter on the bright pink boulder of her rock garden.

Then she whirled on her heel and stomped to the locust tree. He could have grabbed her. Hell, he was burning to grab her arm and bellow a huge WTF at her. But he'd learned long ago to not touch a woman when angry. He was too big and too strong. It was too easy to hurt people when he didn't mean to.

So he let her go and just stood there fuming. He heard the slam of her back door and a sudden loud drumming of African music booming through the house. When the hell had she gotten speakers that capable? He didn't remember seeing them in the house.

Meanwhile, he packed up his tools. Screw it if she—

Thunk.

He turned to see the edge of the ladder back in place. Crossing over, he saw the other woman standing there as she stabilized the ladder. Tori's same blond hair and blue eyes looked up at him, but this woman was taller than Tori and had a more severe presentation. Tighter skirt, shoulders that were squarer, less feminine, and hair and makeup that screamed professional.

Definitely not Tori, but close enough to be related to her. Probably a sister.

"Thanks," he said, doing his best not to sound surly.

"Yeah, sorry about Tori. She's feeling touchy right now. I blame Edward."

He made it to the bottom of the ladder and turned to her. "Ex being a dick?"

"Ex needs to shit or get off the pot. If they're breaking up, then fine. But he needs to stop hanging around. If he's going to hang around, then the dick needs to propose." She looked back at the house. "That's why I took her out for girl time. I thought she'd vent, get all pretty, and then go find herself a real man. Instead, she gets all pissy and takes it out on you." She stood back, frowning as she looked at him. "Why do you look familiar?"

He ducked his head and shrugged. "Dunno. So you're her sister?"

"Yeah. Jessica Williams. Pleased to meet you."

"I'm Mike. Former roofer." He shook her hand then grabbed the ladder to take it back to his uncle's truck.

"You're the guy who's house-sitting, right? The one who caught her when she fell off the roof." She shuddered. "I can't thank you enough for that."

"Right place, right time."

"Well thank God for that. Tori needs a keeper."

Mike shrugged, beginning to be irritated by the way this

woman dismissed her own sister. "Renovating a house is a big job."

"No shit, but she gets these wild hairs when everyone knows she can't handle it. We live in terror of what she's going to do next. Once when she was a kid—"

"Shouldn't you be talking to her? I mean she's obviously upset."

Jessica laughed, the sound brittle. "I'm the one she told to fuck off first. You were just in the vicinity to get her second volley."

Then before Mike could respond to that, Jessica frowned at the side of his uncle's van. Roof Doc blazed in large letters along with a bright red cross over a black roof.

"Look, I know Tori's touchy, but I'm afraid she's going to kill herself." She pulled a wallet out of her purse and peeled off four hundred dollar bills. "Do whatever you can to finish her roof. She's got a yoga class she goes to most mornings."

Geez, what the hell was it about these people? They kept throwing money at him. "It's her house. I can't work on it without her permission."

"I know, but I'm worried sick."

He shook his head. "She's doing fine on the roof on her own."

"Except when she falls off."

Well, she had a point there, but he still wasn't taking her money. "Why don't you offer her the cash? She can hire me if she wants."

"I already have, but she won't take it. I had to strong arm her into the facial and hair appointment." She pulled another hundred out of her purse. "Come on. Just do it. Contrary to her little fit there, she likes you. You can convince her to let you work." She grabbed his hand and pressed the bills into his palm. He could have avoided it, but she didn't seem like the kind of woman to take no for an answer without a fight. There were better ways to deal with this particular problem. And now that he was thinking more clearly, he knew what to do.

So he held up the money before her, giving her the opportunity to take it back.

"I'm just going to give this to Tori. Let her decide."

"Just be charming when you do it." She glanced back at the house as the drum beats ratcheted up another notch. "But I'd wait until she switches to something less tribal."

He was about to say something. He was the last person to get in between sisters, but she had to know that throwing money at a stranger was the wrong way to handle things. Except the moment he started to talk to her, she looked at her watch.

"Oh shit. I've got to get to O'Hare. Here's my card—" She handed that to him. "Call me and let me know how it goes. I can cover any other reasonable roofing expense as well. But make sure to keep it reasonable."

She pointed a finger at him for emphasis, then softened it with a laugh. Jesus, she was acting as if she'd just given her assistant an order. Then she rushed back to her sedan and peeled out of the driveway.

Which is when he headed over to Tori's. Tribal music be damned. Her friends and family were all nutcases. He was going to throw her sister's money at her and wash his hands of the lot of them.

Chapter Five

Tori was taking great satisfaction in slamming down floor tiles and banging them in place with a specially designed rubber mallet. Her expensive salon hairstyle was now gone, pulled back into a ponytail that didn't get into her eyes. And as for the hundreds of dollars of makeup that her sister had convinced her to buy? They were thrown into the lowest drawer in her bathroom. She might look at it again next millennium.

Which is when she was stopped by the appearance of a pair of big basketball feet right in front of where she was about to hammer. She was still deciding how to react when five crisp hundred dollar bills floated down.

She looked up in confusion.

He said, "*Garble burble* your sister."

With a grunt, she pushed up from her knees and crossed to the stereo she'd just stolen back from Edward. She flicked it off but the sudden silence seemed to pound in her ears louder than the drum beats.

Finally she took a breath. "What did you say?"

"That's from your sister. She says you need to hire a

professional roofer."

She rolled her eyes. "Jess says a lot of things. And like good little minions, we're all supposed to fall in line." Then she flopped down on a chair and wiped away the sweat on her forehead, no doubt smearing her expensive liquid pearl foundation in the process. "Thank you for trying to help with the roof, but—"

"You don't need any help. I got that."

She swallowed. The anger in his voice was clear, but he wasn't stomping around in a fit like Edward would. He was just standing there with his big feet and his broad shoulders. He wasn't even saying anything, but she felt guilty for yelling at him earlier. It wasn't his fault her sister was a bossy know-it-all who drove her insane.

"Sorry I snapped at you," she finally said. Then she looked back down at the pile of money. "I'm surprised she didn't hit you up for an endorsement deal or something."

"She didn't recognize me." He sounded a little miffed about that.

"People don't expect a multi-millionaire to be roofing someone else's house." Then she grinned, feeling evil for the petty revenge. "She's going to kick herself when she finds out who you really are."

"What does she do?"

"Mergers and acquisitions in New York." She pitched her voice high, imitating her sister at the woman's most pompous. "Never underestimate the appearance of status. A woman who looks like a million bucks is going to be valued at a million bucks." She jumped up from her chair and stomped to the kitchen for a glass of ice water. "Jesus, do I look like someone who wears Valentino pumps? My department chair is happy when I don't show up barefoot."

"You go to school barefoot? In Chicago?"

"Never." Then she leaned back against the refrigerator.

"But you know, boots get hot. I kick them off. The kids do, too." She sounded like a three-year-old. Joey ate a bug so I did, too. She sighed. "Keep the money. Consider it payment for catching me out of the air."

"Bullshit. That's your money and you can do what you want with it."

She frowned at him. "You kept Edward's hundred."

He grinned. "That's 'cause I won our bet."

God he looked great when he grinned. She'd watched some clips of his basketball games on YouTube. He shaved his hair during the season and showed off a tat on the back of his head that looked like a tribal eagle. But now he was on break, so his hair was growing in thick and dark. A tight skull cap of barely an inch long, but it drew her gaze in the way it framed his face. Cut square across his forehead, it made the angles of his cheeks and jaw seem crisp and hard. When he'd stomped in here, his brows had been lowered in anger and his jaw clenched tight.

Scary on a man his size. But when she'd looked into his eyes, she'd seen a patient intelligence. Not that she was the best judge of character, but that didn't seem to matter. Even when his hands were clenched, all she had to do was look in his eyes and she'd relax. She had nothing to fear from him because he wasn't a man to let his emotions run away with him.

Which meant he was darkly attractive when angry. But now that his grin softened the harsh cut of his face, his whole demeanor seemed to lift. Fortunately, the crow's feet kept him from appearing too movie-star handsome. But that was nothing compared to what she saw in his eyes.

This time the intelligence shifted to something devilish. Part mischief, part seduction, and filled with challenge. He was daring her to join him. Not just in the laughter, but in something much more. She wasn't a competitive person.

Challenges usually left her bored. But this was a temptation. *He* was a temptation, and that was a wholly new experience.

"Do you know why I was given this house?" she asked. As usual, her words had only a vague relationship to what she was thinking.

He shook his head.

"Aunt Mabel married a dreamer. Uncle Bob never followed through on anything. He was smart and had really good ideas, but he never accomplished anything because he could never focus long enough to finish it."

"Hard man to live with," he said, and he sounded like he knew.

"They had two kids, Sam and Robbie. Both have good careers and live elsewhere. She could have sold the house and split the money between them. Uncle Bob died years ago of heart disease, so he wasn't a factor."

"But she gave the house to you. Why?"

Tori looked down at the empty glass in her hand. She could still see the words typed in clear black letters. "Her will said that the house goes to me because *every dreamer needs a place to call home*."

"She called you a dreamer?" He sounded shocked. As if he couldn't believe it. "Don't you have a PhD? A year with the Dalai Lama and all that?"

She looked at him, startled that he could wonder at the word. "My whole family calls me a space cadet. Dreamer is the nicest—"

"Well, then I wish my cousins were ditzes. Jesus, no wonder you want to rip this house up from top to bottom."

He understood. When everyone else in her life was treating her like a two-year-old out on a dangerous daydream, he understood exactly what was driving her. This was her house now. And she would fucking prove to everyone what she could do.

He stood up and crossed into her kitchen. He grabbed a glass and headed for the tap, but she gestured to the refrigerator. "There's homemade lemonade in there, but it's kind of tart." She shrugged. "I forgot to buy sugar."

He paused. "How tart?"

She held up her own glass. "I'm drinking water."

"Water it is."

"I was going to buy beer for you, but I don't know what kind you like—"

"I'm not picky."

"—so I bought a variety. Thought I'd start experimenting. Edward always called it a blue collar drink, but I was surprised at how much some of it costs."

"Edward doesn't know shit." He opened her refrigerator and let out a low whistle. "When you experiment, you don't go halfway, do you?"

She looked over. She'd bought one bottle of thirty-two different brands of beer. She hadn't even started on the cans, but this was every brand the small liquor store had. "It was a whim."

"I'm not complaining. So which one do you want to try first?"

She didn't understand what he meant but then he gestured to the beer array.

"I've become a little stuck in my beer choices too," he continued. "Why don't we split the bottles? Expand our palates together?"

She thought about it for a second, her gaze slipping to the five hundred dollar bills on the floor. "The World Beer Cup competition has over ninety categories of beer. And beeradvocate.com has reviews of over thirty-two thousand different labels."

"Sounds like you've done some research."

She smiled. "My whims always get a thorough Google

search. Anything else would just be lazy."

"Of course."

She grinned. "I think five hundred dollars can buy a lot of beer."

He looked to the bills and laughed. "I think your sister would consider a thorough understanding of alcohol is just as important as a new roof."

"Only if we bought really expensive beer."

"I'm pretty sure that can be arranged."

"I'm pretty sure I'd like to start with that German one with the guy who looks like Uncle Bob on the label."

He looked in and picked it up. "St. Bernardus Prior 8. I've never seen a beer bottle with a cork before."

She picked up her phone. "Should I check the ratings first?"

"Of course not," he said in mock outrage. "A proper experiment should try to eliminate bias."

"I completely agree."

He unwound the metal and worked out the cork as he crossed to her side. Then he wrapped his hand around hers—the one that was holding her empty glass—and tilted it to the side enough to pour the beer in carefully. She watched the dark liquid roll smoothly into her glass, but her thoughts were on the heat of his hand around hers. The strength in his fingers and the way he seemed to cradle her hand even as he guided it exactly as he wanted.

Heat expanded in her belly. The slow simmer of attraction that had been present for days heated up a notch. She looked up into his face, so large and so opposite from everyone else in her world. How could she feel so comfortable with someone so different?

He noticed her look and smiled back at her and again she saw that twinkle of deviltry in his eyes. No one challenged her like that, with an expression that said *I see you looking at me.*

Want to play?

She did. She really did.

So when he released her hand to pour the rest of the bottle into his glass, she licked her lips. She settled into that warming burn of attraction and decided to let it go as it wanted. A flash fire of wild abandon or a steadily increasing want. Either way was fine with her.

He set the bottle on the counter, then dropped down beside her on the floor. She was still in a chair, but he was so large, his head nearly made it up to hers. Then he held up his glass.

"Let the experiment begin," he said.

"Carpe Beer," she said. Then at his look, she shrugged. "It's something I saw on a student's T-shirt."

"Carpe Beer," he echoed.

Then together they drank.

A lot.

...

The beer was good and in plentiful quantity. They were splitting beers, but she was pouring the lion's share into his glass. If he didn't know better, he might think she was trying to get him drunk, but he didn't care. He was having too good a time talking with her.

He loved the random way her mind worked. They'd be talking about basketball one second then she'd be off on bees, comparing basketball plays to the lifecycle of a hive. It made no sense, but it had them both laughing because from a certain drunken perspective, it was completely logical.

She got him to talk about his childhood in Detroit. He'd barely known his father except that he was a gambler, but his uncle was the best. And his stepdad was a close second. She liked her father because he was as air-headed as she was—her words, not his. Her mother, sister, and older brother were the psycho driven ones. Which started him talking about his not-driven cousins—freeloaders every one of them—and pretty soon she was off on the child-rearing habits of Aborigines and how it related to their religion.

He loved it.

Then they started talking about weird relatives. That took them through the next five beers. Then came another Aunt Mabel story. He'd just finished talking about his great uncle the hoarder who'd died before they had a name for hoarding when she'd lurched forward and said in a husky whisper, "Guess what I found in my aunt's bathroom."

Given what he'd already learned about her family, he couldn't begin to guess, but he did anyway. "A worm farm?"

"No, Uncle Bob sold that off years ago."

He blinked at her. "Seriously?"

"Well, he sold off the property. The worms had already died."

"So no farm, then."

"Nope. Condoms."

He paused in the middle of draining his glass. "What?"

"Yup. She bought them two months before she died."

"No kidding." He already knew the woman had died of cancer, so to be frisky at the end was unusual.

"Yup. I think she had a boyfriend. I think he took her to chemo. Which, you know, is really sweet."

"Do you know who it was?"

She shook her head. "Only that two of the condoms were missing." Then she started laughing. It began as a snort, but eventually became a real laugh that she didn't try to hold back. She'd long since abandoned the chair to sprawl on the floor beside him. Now she fell against his shoulder, holding her arms to her belly.

"You really think she got it on with her guy?" he asked,

loving the feel of her whole body shaking in laughter.

"I hope so," she said. "I really do."

She looked at him then. She rolled her face toward him, right there on his shoulder. Her lips were cherry red, her eyes sparkling blue pools. And a thought formed in his brain: she was so different than the women he usually met. Basketball bunnies had no subtlety. But Tori? She was different. She was amazing.

"Tori?"

"Hmmm?" She smiled up at him, and he had trouble focusing on anything but the dark red of her lips.

"Are you trying to seduce me?"

She giggled, but she didn't look away. "Maybe. Am I doing it badly?"

"Nope." He'd been rock hard and aching for her by the second beer. "But we're both drunk." So much for everything in moderation, but he'd been having too much fun to stop. "I don't want you regretting anything in the morning."

She thought about it for a moment, but when she spoke, her words were crystal clear. "Can I tell you a secret?"

He grinned. "Sure."

"I never regret anything. Ever. People try to make me regret things. They tell me how I was stupid or not thinking or something. Usually they're right, so I pretend to be sad so they'll go away. But really and truly, I never regret anything."

He tried to imagine living like that. Never looking back and wishing you could do it all over again. He averaged three regrets a game. A moment where he'd made the wrong choice or had been too slow or too stupid. He obsessed over his mistakes, endlessly replaying them in his mind at night. Had that choice cost them the game? The championship?

Those regrets were just the basketball ones. Sometimes he thought he obsessed over those because it was too hard to think about the other choices. The life choices where he hurt someone or forgot something or… Damn. There were a million.

"Not a single regret?" he pressed. "Really?"

"I've been stupid. Lots. I'm not even sure a year with the Dalai Lama was the right choice."

"That can't be true."

"Gave up an internship with the Gates Foundation."

Okay, so maybe there were choices there. Career paths that could have gone one way or another.

"But regret doesn't change the choice. It just distracts me from the cool things right in front of me now." She set her hand on his chest, small and so white. He took it in his, wrapping her fingers around two of his. White on brown. Small and large.

Lust surged through him, hard and hot and…

"We're drunk, Tori. We can't—"

"No regrets."

"For you, baby," he said as he pressed his mouth to hers. Just one kiss. One slow, drugging taste. And maybe a little more. After all, what was one more regret to him?

She kissed him back with her whole body. Not just her mouth and tongue, but her breasts as she arched into him, and her hands as they roved across his chest. She clutched at him and would have climbed on top of him if she'd had the angle.

"Whoa, baby," he said, trying to hold her back. His heart was pounding and the need to take her was nearly overwhelming. But he was a big man and he'd learned to be careful with his strength. "Wait a second."

She was licking along his jaw, nibbling up to his ear. The feel was hot and wet and made his fingers clench in hunger, but her pace was too fast, her need almost frantic. So this time he did use his strength. He grabbed her shoulders and gently set her back from him.

The look of her dazed eyes and red wet lips weakened

his resolve. But then she blinked and focused on him. "I'm of German descent," she said.

He almost chuckled. "Another non-sequitur?"

"I process alcohol very quickly." Then when he didn't answer, she huffed and pulled the tie out of her hair, letting the straight blond hair drop around her shoulders. God she was beautiful and he wanted her more than he wanted his next breath.

Meanwhile, she pressed her head against his shoulder. Her breath was warm where it cascaded over his chest and he wrapped her tight in his arms.

"Tori—" he groaned.

"Will you wait here? Just for five minutes?"

What could he say to that? Of course he'd wait. He was dying to know what she'd do next.

Chapter Six

Tori spit out the toothpaste, rinsed her mouth, and then took a good long look at herself in the mirror. She absently noted that her cheeks were flushed, and her hair was a mess. But rather than focus on those trivialities, she stared into her own eyes and did something she absolutely hated to do: she thought about what she was about to do.

As a rule, she hated weighing pros and cons, thinking her actions through, and all that ponderous head stuff. Her mind was better suited to philosophy and comparative religions. Ask her to describe the different myths attached to the Egyptian god Set, and she could recite them from memory. Ask her to plan her next week, and she was hopeless.

Ask her to decide exactly what she wanted to do with her next door neighbor, and she broke out into a cold sweat. But not thinking about her relationships is how she'd ended up with Edward for so many years. It was time to change that pattern. Besides, she got the feeling that Mike was worth the extra work.

So she thought.

She thought about the way his eyes crinkled when he laughed. And that he laughed often with her. She thought about running her hands down his entire ripped torso—front and back—and seeing if she could name every single muscle as it popped under her fingers. She thought about how very big he was, and yet she didn't feel dwarfed or stifled around him. If anything, he was too careful—physically—with her and she found that really sweet.

She tried to think of the cons, and frankly there was one really big one. He was a sports god and she was clueless. Worse, she thought what he did for a living was shortsighted. Who picked such an unstable career? Forget being too old by age forty. One twisted ankle—or a torn rotator cuff—and he was out of work for the rest of his life. It was nuts, and by extension that made him nuts.

And yet...she still liked him. She still wanted him. She still—

"Tori? You okay in there?"

"Um. Yeah. Just a second." She hurriedly flushed the toilet then rinsed her hands, splashing water on her face as an extra boost. It was what she always did when she started thinking in the bathroom and took too long.

A quick brush through her hair and she opened the bathroom door to see him leaning against the wall right outside the door, a look of wariness in his eyes. He scanned her from head to toe and then opened his mouth to say something. She didn't give him the chance.

"I want a rebound boyfriend."

He blinked at her, his gaze turning laser sharp. And he didn't say a damned thing. Which was really uncomfortable.

So rather than face his weird expression, her mind skittered away to something irrelevant. "Wait. That's a basketball reference, isn't it?"

"Yes," he said slowly. "It is."

Nothing more. Damn, this was harder than she thought. Most men usually didn't require so much thought on her part. They needed little prompting to fill the conversation, but he actually listened to her which required her to say intelligent things or explain herself. That was harder than it should be, but she gave it a shot anyway.

"I've decided I want a boyfriend to help me get over Edward."

"Do you need help getting over Edward?"

She swallowed. No, not really. "Maybe," she hedged. "Maybe I need to experience other men."

"That would require more than one man. And not a boyfriend, which implies a commitment. Or at least exclusivity."

Good point. "I've tried sleeping around. It wasn't nearly as fun as it sounds."

His eyebrows rose at that even as he relaxed backward against the wall. "That's something we have in common then," he said in the way she sometimes said things that weren't on point, but filled the silence while she thought of something else to say.

And yet she was pretty curious about that. "So you've slept around?" Then she winced. Of course he slept around. All she had to do was Google his name and a zillion images of him appeared. Take out the game shots, and she got to see his women. At least a dozen different ones in the last year alone.

Meanwhile, he managed to shrug without moving his hurt shoulder. "I had some wild days."

She nodded as if her wildness could even remotely compare to his. But whatever. "I explored during my freshman year in college. There were lots of opportunities."

He chuckled. "I explored up through my freshman year in the NBA."

"Bet you had more fun than I did."

He chuckled. "This is one area in which I have no interest in competing."

Right. Back to the point. "So I figure you're next door until your shoulder heals, right? Then it's back to the east coast."

He nodded.

"And I'll go back to teaching in the fall. So for the summer…" She tilted her head. "Would you prefer we call it a summer fling?"

"No."

Oh. Right. "You hate this idea."

"I'm still trying to understand your idea. How about you try again in plain, simple words?"

She took a breath. Simple declarative sentences. She could do that. "Why won't you sleep with me? Aren't you attracted to me?" Oops. Those were questions, not statements.

"Yes. And because we're drunk."

She huffed out a breath, managing to poof the fine hairs that danced around her face. She brushed them away in irritation. "I'm getting more sober by the second."

"I'm not."

She waited for him to say more, but he remained stubbornly silent. So she folded her arms and leaned back against the wall in the exact mirror of his position.

"I'm attracted to you but I don't want a permanent fixture in my life." She shuddered at that. Edward had become like a heavy antique desk in her life. Too big to move and too expensive to throw out. Not without burning down the entire house. Which is basically what she'd done when she'd moved here.

"So you're looking for someone temporary."

"Aren't you? I saw an interview that said you don't intend to settle down with a woman until after your career. Is that wrong?"

He didn't answer that question exactly. Instead, he shifted his feet to stand more upright off the wall. "I'm not looking for anyone at all, Tori."

Oh. Shit. "I, um, I thought with the kisses and everything that you were interested. At least on a just-for-now basis. Which is basically where I live, especially in the summer, so I thought it would work." She sighed, unaccountably depressed. "I guess I'll just find someone else. Thanks anyway."

She started to move away from him. In her mind, this humiliating conversation was over, but before she took more than one step, he was suddenly right there in front of her. Practically looming over her.

"Mike?"

"How are you going to find this someone else?"

She shrugged. She hadn't really given it much thought. Her mind had centered on him. But there were all the usual places. "Bars, I guess. Someplace downtown. I know too many people in Evanston to shop here."

She felt a sudden flare of tension in him. A silent anger that hit her uncomfortably on a visceral level. "You can't just pick up guys in a bar."

Actually that was something she definitely knew she could do. She looked at him, making sure her thoughts were clear on her face.

He sighed. "I mean, obviously you can, but you shouldn't. It's dangerous."

"I'm tired of this conversation," she said rather than argue with him. God, she hated it when people told her what she could and couldn't do. Since he was blocking access to the kitchen, she spun around and started for her bedroom. "It was an idea. If you don't like it, no problem. I'll just—"

"Do what you want anyway," he said. He grabbed her arm, and this time his hands weren't as gentle as before. They were big and hot against her body, and they held her in place as surely as iron shackles. "Tori, listen to me."

She stopped, startled that the idea of shackles with this man was intriguing. She had no objection to being restrained and pleasured, but would he let her chain him up? Would he—

"You are the oddest woman I've ever met," he said.

She smiled. "I count my novelty as an asset."

"Yeah, I can tell."

She laughed. Not many people realized she cultivated her air of odd insouciance, especially around new acquaintances. If they didn't flow with her from the start, she saw no reason to invest time in building a friendship. It was the rare person who enjoyed her odd sense of humor. And no one besides him realized she acted this way on purpose. Or at least she exaggerated her natural tendencies on purpose. Some things slipped out of her mouth even when she was trying to be on her best behavior.

Meanwhile, he was studying her face again. She got the impression he did that with all his opponents. Narrowed his eyes, tilted his head slightly, and looked at them with an intensity that she should find uncomfortable. Instead, she found it rather thrilling. Who in her life had ever looked at her that closely? No one. And—

"Aren't you afraid I'll break your heart?" he asked. "Come fall?"

She laughed, which probably came out more insulting than she intended. His face hardened, and she rushed to explain. "Look, we have nothing in common. I find you fascinating now, but not many things—even people—hold my attention for long."

"You've got a PhD. Doesn't that take years? So that means something has held your attention for a good long time."

True. "But not people. I'm just not wired that way."

He straightened, his expression crying "bullshit" as clearly as if she were telling him the sky was green. "How many years were you with Edward?"

"Too many. And I was bored long ago, but too lazy to leave. My fault. Now I know." She smiled. "Think of it as built-in obsolescence."

"What if you break my heart?"

She blinked. "You can't be serious."

"What, guys don't have hearts?"

"Guys do. You don't. Your own words in that interview. Until your career is done, you've given yourself body, mind, and soul to basketball. Are you saying your heart isn't included in that list?"

He looked uncomfortable and so she knew she was right. Time to press her advantage.

"So you don't want a real girlfriend any more than I want a real boyfriend." She touched his chest, spreading her fingers out and covering a small fraction of the area there. He was a big powerful guy, and the sight of her tiny hand there had her thinking of other places she could put her small hand. And wondering if he was super big there, too. "I want to go to bed with you, Mike," she confessed, her tone more of a whisper. "There wasn't much thought beyond that."

"But with no strings. Separating as soon as the season begins."

She nodded. "And hopefully with some awesome memories."

He shifted his hand to cover hers on his chest. He totally engulfed her, surrounding her all the way up past her wrist.

"Do smart people get drunk different than dumb ones? Like some weird PhD drunk? Coming up with weird ideas when blitzed?"

"Well, of course we do. How do you think I came up with my thesis project?"

He smiled at her, clearly wanting the answer.

"I undertook a thorough study of absinthe in all its

historically accurate forms. By morning, I'd decided that it was directly responsible for certain Egyptian cults and many forms of Bast worship."

He frowned. "Bast?"

She gestured with her chin to the bathroom. "That's her on the wall. The Cat Goddess." She waited a moment while he looked at the elegant depiction of a regal black cat with a mysterious expression and not-so-mysterious boobs. "Come on. You think any sober person would think of that?"

He had no answer to that, which is usually what happened when she spoke about her research. By the time he was looking back at her, she had stepped tighter into his personal space. Close enough that her forearm and elbow settled against his belly.

"So…want to rebound with me?" she asked.

"There are so many things wrong with that question, I can't even begin."

Disappointment curled through her. Again. But before she could pull away, he started backing her up. He simply started moving forward, forcing her to quickly step backward. Three, seven, ten. Oh! He was backing her into her bedroom.

"Um, what are you doing?" she asked, though she'd already figured it out.

"I'm going to show you how a professional rebounds." Three more steps until her hip bumped into a half-unpacked moving box next to her dresser.

Meanwhile, she was working his words around in her mind. "Um, was that supposed to make sense to me?"

"Jesus, woman, I have no idea. I'm too busy thinking of all the novel things I want to try with you."

"Oh," she said, her mind slipping back to the handcuffs. "Well, that's the other—"

He stopped her words with his tongue. All in all, she decided she was okay with that.

Chapter Seven

Tori was an impatient lover. Mostly because—as her mother often accused—she had the attention span of a gnat. That wasn't exactly true. She'd once read the entire Holy Bible on a Sunday afternoon. But in terms of sexual arousal, her interest often waned quickly. She'd learned early that guys got annoyed when she suddenly wanted to look up esoteric facts in the middle of sex. So she'd started going through the act as fast as possible before her mind wandered somewhere else.

Her partners usually didn't mind. Edward especially had been all about thrust, release and here's your vibrator, honey, in case you're feeling neglected. Though in all fairness, he'd been happy to hold the vibrator for her if she wanted.

Mike was an entirely different kind of man.

He didn't start with stripping her naked. In her experience, that was the first order of business for most men. Especially when they were as aroused as Mike obviously was. No clothing could hide an erection that large, and he was in thin jeans. Plus, her hand was right there, stroking downward over the heat.

She only managed to do it once before he caught her fingers and drew it to his lips. He kissed her fingers, then stayed still, obviously debating something in his mind.

"Mike—"

He leaned forward, kissing her lightly. She expected to be slammed onto the bed, but he just licked her lips, nipped at the edges, and then eventually sealed her mouth with his.

In short, he was a slow lover, and she was terrified that she'd insult him when her mind wandered elsewhere. So she broke away and stripped off her tee. She would have taken everything off if her legs hadn't been entwined with his. "You don't have to go slow, Mike. It's okay."

He chuckled. "I've never heard a woman say that before." Then he sobered. "I'm a big guy, Tori. I want to make sure you're fully involved before we do this."

She winced, realizing what he meant: the slow build to a great climax. Except she just wasn't built that way. "Um, I never get fully involved in anything. At least not for long."

He smiled. "That sounds like a challenge."

Oh shit. Not what she meant. He was a competitor and if she put up a goal, he would go through hell and high water to meet it. But he couldn't with her, and he was too perceptive for her to fake it effectively.

"I'm just not wired for slow," she said. "I distract too easily."

He smiled and let his hands trail down her sides, making her shiver. "Good information there. I'll need to work for your attention." He grinned, his white teeth showing brilliantly against his caramel skin. "Good thing I'm used to electrifying millions of people."

"That's in basketball—oh… That's…nice." He was tracing one finger around her nipple. It was even through her bra, but she felt it like a lightning bolt through her belly. But then he kept doing it, adding in a pinch occasionally to the circling motion. Over and over until her sight fuzzed out and she began thinking about what he'd said.

Just exactly how large was he? She tried to think back to her other lovers. She didn't remember any of them as particularly big, so did that mean…

He touched her chin and she blinked, focusing back on him. Oh shit. She'd just dazed out on him.

"Mike, I…um…"

He touched her lips with his thumb, pressing them closed. "That was just a baseline, Tori. I wanted to see what you did when you got bored."

"I wasn't bored," she lied.

He chuckled. "Yes, you were. I only have one rule: don't lie to me."

She swallowed. It wasn't like she lied as a general rule, but guys' egos were fragile. Especially in the lovemaking department. "I—"

"You're going to have to learn to trust me on this. My ego can handle it."

She didn't believe him. She wanted to, but honestly, he was a superstar athlete. He was used to being the best at everything, especially anything physical. And he'd probably had women telling him he was the greatest lover ever since high school. No way was he going to like it—

"So what's going on in that head of yours?"

She blinked. Damn it, she'd just spaced out on him again. Normally she could focus better.

"Let me guess," he said with a smile. "You're used to lying to your lovers. Telling them they've rocked your world when actually you were off thinking about Hindu gods or something."

Damn. He was smarter than she'd ever guessed. And she just wasn't up to faking it with him. "Maybe this isn't a good idea."

He leaned forward, nuzzling along her neck, his words a low rumble against her skin. "Maybe you need to let me try." He licked the skin just behind her ear and she shivered. "Don't worry," he said as his large right hand squeezed her thigh. "I'm just getting the lay of the land here. We're not even close to the main event."

"But that's the problem," she whispered, her eyes drifting closed as she felt his breath heat where he'd nibbled. "I'm not made for long games. It's not your fault—"

"It's nobody's fault, Tori." He pulled back enough that he looked directly into her eyes. "It's just a new challenge, that's all."

His hand slid up underneath her shorts. His fingers were long as they kneaded higher and higher on her thighs. God that felt good. Really good.

She wondered how she was going to get her shorts off. Did she push his hands away now? Did she unbutton the jeans or should she start to undress him?

"Tori," he whispered, and her eyes abruptly riveted back on his.

Oh shit. Her mind had wandered off again. Jesus, she was terrible at this.

"Don't think so much," he said.

"Easy for you to say."

"Look into my eyes."

She was. She had been. Oh wait, maybe she hadn't been. She frowned, trying to think.

He quickly nipped her nose, then moved back such that she looked right into his eyes. "Whenever you leave me, your eyes slide away. Forget the not lying rule. My one rule is this: you look at me."

"I was."

"Look directly into my eyes and I'll look straight into yours. We're going to hold this connection the whole time."

"The whole time?" She wasn't sure that was possible.

"It's a challenge, Tori. Aren't you up for it?"

No. Yes. Maybe. Taunting never worked on her. She lived too much in her own world to allow silly tricks like that to influence her choices. And yet suddenly she was feeling competitive. She wanted to prove to him that she could do so simple a thing. At least she could do it longer than he could.

So she lifted her chin. "Fine," she whispered. "Have it your way. I won't lie to you. I'll look you in the eye the whole time. And when the whole experience sucks, I'm not going to sugarcoat it."

He grinned as if she'd just given him a championship trophy. "Game on." And then he scooped her up in his good arm. Or at least he tried to. Mostly he was pulling her tight against him while she was busy squeaking in alarm. She instinctively grabbed his shoulders. His broad, strong, muscular shoulders. Nice. But she'd broken eye contact.

Shit.

"That doesn't count," she said. "You surprised me."

He adjusted her easily in his grip such that they were eye to eye. "Fair enough," he said. "Now is the bed clear or is there bad stuff under all those clothes? I can't see around the boxes."

Right. Looking around, she remembered her bedroom was a disaster. Half-unpacked boxes everywhere, the clothes her sister had forced on her were on the bed, and God only knew what else was strewn about the floor. "Um, the bed's clear. Just clothes."

"Do you mind if we wrinkle them?"

She grinned at the idea of exactly what her sister would say to that. "Not in the least."

"Excellent. And you need to look at me, remember?"

Damn it. "You weren't looking at me," she said defensively.

"I was making sure not to accidentally shove you against

that box of…spoons?"

"My aunt's collection. I'm packing it up for Goodwill. They're supposed to be valuable but I'm not sure I have the patience to sell them."

He set her gently back against the bed. She was the one who collapsed onto the mattress while he dropped to his knees before her. He was so tall that even kneeling on the floor he almost looked her eye to eye. Then before she could say more, he stroked his thumb across her jaw. "Are you nervous, Tori?"

She never got nervous. It just wasn't in her nature. But now that he mentioned it… "I've never had a sex challenge before."

He grinned. "Me either. So it's okay if we fail."

She stiffened. "I have no intention of failing." It was pure bravado, but his grin widened. There was little light in here except for the moonlight that spilled in from the window and the eco bulbs in the hallway. It lit the room well enough, but the shadows on his face seemed to emphasize his expression. It made his smile brighter and his eyes luminous.

"So kiss me."

She leaned in, but then she started to close her eyes. "I can't do it with my eyes open."

"Right." His expression grew mischievous. "Then how about you watch me?"

He stroked her arms, his fingers so light, she wondered if she was imagining the soft brush of his skin against hers. But the heat that began to simmer just beneath her skin was proof enough. He was watching her eyes as he did it. Their gazes caught and held even as he slipped his thumbs across her belly. Her knees weakened and her breath grew short. Her nipples were painfully tight and he hadn't even gone near them yet. Oh wow. She was burning up.

"Don't close your eyes," he said and it took a moment for her to realize that her eyes had been drifting shut.

"Then let me touch you." She didn't wait for an answer, but grabbed hold of his shirt and tugged. Good thing he ducked for her because he was too tall for her to do it sitting. And then his chest was right there before her, crisp hairs darkening the center and highlighting the line down to his groin.

"Up here," he said. And again, she had to think a moment before she remembered to look into his eyes.

"You gotta let me look at you," she said.

He shook his head.

"Then you can't look either."

A flash of chagrin crossed his features, but then he shook his head again. "See me with your fingertips."

She rolled her eyes. "Come on, Mike. This doesn't make sense."

"I haven't got anything you haven't seen before." Then his grin widened. "Though as a rule I am rather impressive."

"So let me—"

He leaned forward, unhooking her bra with quick fingers. "If I can't look, then you can't either."

"So look."

"I'd rather feel."

Apparently, he'd rather feel a lot. He didn't even wait for her bra to drop away but slid his hands forward to cup her breasts. Big hands on medium breasts meant that she felt as if he were surrounding her. His fingers were endlessly dexterous, manipulating her body in ways that astounded her. He first just lifted them up, then he began to play. Moving and shifting his hands, stroking across her skin or kneading her with fingers that pushed deep into her muscles.

She was nearly frantic for him to touch her nipples, which he finally did a few moments later. He thumbed the peaks first, before twisting them. Her back was arching, her body flushed and the throb in her womb was nothing short of stunning. She'd never been this aroused before. She hadn't even thought it was possible.

And all the while their eyes held. She knew she was flushed, her lips parted as her breaths grew shallow and quick. But what she saw in his eyes was no less erotic than what his hands were doing. He was focused on her. There was delight in his eyes as he played with her breasts. And a joyous kind of triumph too. She wanted to tease him about his ego, but she hadn't the focus. And besides, he deserved the credit. He was really good at this.

Her hands were clutching his shoulders, digging in as she held herself up. But now she wanted to do this to him. She wanted to know if she could make him so hungry for her he thought of nothing else. And so she leaned down and fumbled at his jeans. She couldn't manage the button, but she was able to tug at the belt loops, encouraging him to stand up so she could handle him for real.

"Damn it," she muttered, her gaze going downward.

"I got it," he said, as he left her body to grab hold of her hands. That wasn't at all what she wanted, but he didn't let go of her hands or stand up either. He just held her.

"Mike?" she said, her gaze going back up to his.

"There you are," he said. "I'm going to stop everything whenever you look away."

"I'm going to make sure you're so involved you forget about my eyes."

He chuckled and she knew that he had accepted her challenge. Well then. This was a game she intended to win. She waited while he finally stood up and released his jeans. His very impressive erection jutted forward. She saw it in her peripheral vision. Then she lifted away his boxer briefs and pushed everything down. Finally, she could touch him. And wow. There was a lot of him to touch.

Long, thick, and pulsing in her hands. She felt the wetness on the mushroom head, rolled her thumb around in it, and then gently squeezed him. It would take more than her hand to enfold the full length of him, but she didn't need to touch everything at once. It was enough to grip him and alternate the pressure of her fingers. Especially since she saw his eyes flutter as she did it. And then she tightened her hold and slid down to his base.

She felt the spring of his hair against the back of her hand, but mostly she felt him thrust as she gripped him. His low growl of hunger had her grinning. Though, he hadn't lost his connection with her gaze.

And while she continued to explore his reactions to her movements, he easily undid her shorts and pushed them and her panties to the floor. Then they both kicked their clothes aside. Which meant they were naked. She had an NBA star right in front her, a man cut so beautifully that Michelangelo couldn't have sculpted better. And she couldn't look. She couldn't feast her sight on every glorious inch of him. So she'd have to do it with her hands.

She touched him. Every part of him that she could reach. Every ripple, every bulging muscle and the sweet valleys in between. She teased his nipples, she feathered her fingers through his hair, and she made sure to keep her eyes on his even when she stretched down to squeeze his sac. She watched as his jaw tightened and his nostrils flared. And she felt it as his large hands slid over her hips to delve between her thighs.

His fingers were long and quick as they thrust between her folds. She was slick and he had the size to rub up and down over everything while she clenched in reaction.

"Can we take this horizontal?" she asked, startled by how breathless she felt.

"Where are the condoms?" His voice had a gravelly sound to it that thrilled her.

"Bedside table." She gestured with her chin, but didn't break eye contact.

"Got it."

He did. He was tall enough to reach into the drawer and find the box. She broke eye contact first. She didn't remember what else was in there and was pleased to find nothing more than a notepad and the condoms. He had a foil packet out and was rolling it on in record time. She had a moment's unease when she realized that he had obvious practice with the things. That was both reassuring and disturbing all at once. He probably hadn't had to have a sex challenge with any of his other women. But he was her rebound lover, she reminded herself. She didn't care if he'd been with a lot of other women before or after her. It didn't matter even though the very idea hurt a little.

"Tori," he said, drawing her gaze back up to his. "We can go slow."

She laughed. "We've already taken triple my usual time. If we go any slower, I'll fall asleep." It was a lie. She was wide awake and well revved. Unfortunately, she'd forgotten who she was speaking to. He took her words as another challenge.

"Asleep?" he said with mock affront. Suddenly he was pushing her backward such that she dropped flat on the mattress. Then he crawled up over her, caging her with his arms and legs.

"Tori..." he began, but then didn't say more. Was he just speaking her name? Probably. But she read so much more into his tone. *This is the woman I want. The person I'm going to make love with. The woman who—*

She reached up and drew his mouth down to hers. Her thoughts were starting to spin to unwanted places. To words that held more than simple desire. She didn't want to go there. Not with her rebound lover.

He kissed her back with power that left her breathless. All mastery as he thrust inside her mouth, dueled with her tongue, and won in whatever game they were playing. But then he broke the kiss, pulling back as he gazed at her.

He didn't say a word, and she didn't either. Her heart was pounding too fast, her mind trying to grab hold of something but finding only his eyes. His steady, solid gaze as he shifted his legs. With slow, deliberate movements, he pushed a knee between hers. She had no problem with letting him settle between her thighs. When he pushed them wider open, she arched into it, lifting her body toward him.

Then she cradled his hips with her legs as he set himself in place. The latex was cold for a moment, but heated rapidly as he pushed gently inside. Not far. Just a little push and she tried to grip him in reaction. A small push from him, a large "yes" from her as she wrapped her legs around him.

"Don't you want to go faster?" she asked. She was nearly insane with the need to feel him inside her.

His teeth flashed white. "Nope. This is just fine."

Well maybe for him. She was all but weeping with need. She tightened her legs and angled her pelvis. She did it in just the right way, pulling him inside by another inch. God, he felt good. He already stretched her and she liked the feel of it. Like he was staking claim. Especially since he made a sound deep in his throat when he did it. More primal than a groan, and she arched up to nip at his nose.

His eyes widened in surprise and she flashed him a coy grin. "You weren't looking at me."

"I was too."

"Nope. Your attention had wandered somewhere a little further south." She wasn't sure if it was true. She was merely guessing, but he cast her a rueful look.

"Some things are worth appreciating fully." Then he clearly, specifically, held her gaze as he pushed deeper in.

Her breath caught, and her eyes fluttered, but she held his eyes. Damn that felt good. That felt *full* and she squeezed him just to prove to herself that she could.

"More," she whispered.

He pushed in and again she squeezed around him. She saw his throat work in reaction, but he didn't go faster.

"Again."

He did. This time it wasn't a smooth slide but more of a jerk. It felt like being pierced slowly and in all the best ways. She arched, trying to force him deeper. She strained and she tightened, but he didn't move.

Then she felt his hand. He was braced on his good arm, and she didn't think he'd have the dexterity with his weaker one. Boy, was she wrong. He shifted it around between them. Together, they were so slick that he could rub her clit in smooth heavy strokes.

"Oh God," she gasped.

She was tightening, her whole body squeezing him. Needing him.

"Please," she cried. She'd never begged for sex in her life, but she wanted it now. She wanted the heavy slam over and over.

She grabbed at his arm, pulling it back, and for once he complied. She was about to demand more when—

Slam. He was fully seated. He added a grind and she saw stars behind her eyes.

"Yes," she whispered.

Finally he began to move like she wanted. Out, then hard in. Again and again, each impact making her cry out. Every time he ground deep against her, sensation rocketed up her spine.

Once more.

Again.

Yes!

She was flying. Her body cascading in pleasure as he became frantic. He slammed against her while she clung to him.

That made it better.

Every slam rocketed her higher. Hotter. Yes! And then…

He growled.

She felt him release. Pulse after pulse as he bucked into her.

And suddenly she was flying again. Tingles. Fireworks. A cascade of *oh yeah!* She experienced it all as she gripped every part of him.

"Holy shit," he gasped as he suddenly collapsed onto her. The weight was nice, the feel of him still pulsing inside was even better. And she was grinning from ear to ear.

"Definitely," she answered. Best sex of her life. She let her eyes drift closed. His face was pressed against her neck, his breath hot against her skin. Eventually it steadied. Eventually while she was still languid beneath him, he pressed into her shoulder. Then he whispered the best post-coital words in the world.

"I closed my eyes."

She giggled. Her eyes had closed, too, but she wasn't going to admit it.

Then he gently disentangled himself, sliding to the side. Then there were more moments of clean up and adjustment. He did it. She just lay there with a goofy grin on her face. And then he settled in beside her, tucking her tight to his chest.

"I promise to do better next time," he said.

"Good," she answered as she snuggled into his arms. "Because I've got some ideas, too…"

She fell asleep to the deep rumble of his laugh.

Chapter Eight

Mike woke to a persistent ache in his shoulder. The pain was enough that it throbbed all the way up to the back of his skull. There were other feelings as well. A warm female body pressed against him, the scent of lemon and sex, and a sweet languor that he hadn't felt in a long time. But it was the shoulder that bothered him, and probably that pain which pushed him to consciousness at barely after dawn.

He tried to shift positions, but the pain sharpened enough that his eyes shot fully open. And then facts started to pile up in his brain.

Tori was sleeping on his shoulder. She was tucked tight against him to the point that his morning wood was already shifting happily against her bottom. As they were both naked, this could have been a very nice way to wake.

But the shoulder pain was growing exponentially now that he was alert enough to process it. Worse, his arm and fingers as they extended beneath her were numb.

Bad. Bad. Bad.

His hands were his life and he'd just cut off blood flow to

them for God only knew how many hours.

His reaction was immediate. He didn't think about it, he just did it and then apologized afterward.

He jerked his arm out from under her and sat up, waiting through the tingling and weakness as life returned painfully to his hand.

And he cursed the whole time.

"Well that's a new way to wake up."

He looked over at Tori, seeing her rosy cheeks, soft sleepy eyes, and bedhead. She was adorable and part of him wanted to try out his returning dexterity on her. But that was the lust-filled part, not the panicking part which dominated right now.

So he turned away and forced himself to mutter a half-surly, "I didn't mean to wake you." He shoved out of bed. "I'll let myself out. You can sleep in."

"No need," she said as she pushed herself up to a slouching sit. She matched him perfectly, except she wasn't rubbing her shoulder. "It's summer break. I can sleep or not however I want." Then she gave him a coy smile. "If I want to stay in bed all day—"

He cut her off before she could finish. "I've got PT and stuff. Sorry."

Her gaze cut to where he was massaging his shoulder. "Can I help?"

"No," he snapped. His hurt arm twitched as he mentally tried to put a leash on his temper. But it was too early in the fucking morning, and she was the reason he was in this position. His shoulder was screwed up because he caught her out of the air. It ached like hot coals because she'd slept on it all night. Who knew what other disaster she might perpetrate in his life?

It wasn't rational, but he wasn't in a thinking place right then. So he pulled on his pants one-handed. It was hard, which only made him more pissed off.

Meanwhile, Tori shifted to her knees, completely unconscious about her nudity. He didn't want to look, but even his angry brain couldn't resist the sight of the dawn light softening as it stroked her breasts with pale color.

"You're really upset," she said softly. Her head tilted to one side and her blond hair slipped down to curtain her shoulder. God, she was beautiful. And in that moment, a choice crystallized before him as stark and clear as if God had put two things in front of him and said, "Pick one."

On the one hand, he had Tori. She was smart, funny, infinitely interesting and hot enough to boil his brain to mush.

On the other hand, he had his career. The demands of pro basketball were increasing and his body required more maintenance. It was a losing game. He was aging. Injuries came more quickly and healing took longer. There were always younger, faster, stronger men ready to step into his place. Which meant stuff that he could ignore ten years ago were now big deals. And Tori was the biggest deal of all.

He could lose a lot of hours with her. He could take risks with his shoulder, shave off training time, and even blow off a practice or two just to be with her. Hell, he already had in some ways. It's not like roofing her house was on his list of recommended activities.

Which meant even a summer fling idea was toast. He couldn't do it and rehab his shoulder.

So there it was: Tori or basketball?

"I'm sorry, Tori. I've got to go."

She nodded, accepting it with calm. "Okay. Want to come over tonight? We still have lots of beer to try."

He shook his head as he grabbed his shirt off the floor. "Thanks, but no. When I said I have to go, I…"

His voice trailed away because she'd stood up from the bed. Her breasts bounced and her sweet ass was within reach as she grabbed a tee and shrugged it on. He wasted precious moments watching everything jiggle. His morning wood was becoming more insistent, but he just stood there watching. And when she bent over to pull on panties, he broke out in a sweat.

What he wouldn't give to step up behind her right then and thrust straight into heaven.

Answer: he wouldn't give up his career.

It seemed like such a small thing. Sex with a hot girl for the summer. But athletics was a game of inches; a pro career was the sum of every single moment spent in training. Or not spent. And he couldn't afford to let things slide. Even for a summer.

So he backed away from her.

One step, then two while she shimmied into her shorts.

He should have run because a moment later she turned around and smiled at him. The expression was sweet and open. He saw no ulterior motive in her look, no greed or lust or anything. Just a hello and I like you.

He liked her right back.

"I can't," he ground out, talking more to his own brain than hers.

"Okay. Not tonight. Tomorrow's good—"

"It's not good," he said, his voice thick, his anxiety ratcheting up another degree. His shoulder pain had eased with the return of blood flow, but the pain throbbed in his mind like a drumbeat. It spelled *doom* over and over until he used it to strengthen his resolve.

"No, Tori," he said as he finally straightened up to his full height before her. He wasn't facing her down; he was squaring off with the steady hammer of fear in his brain. "I'm not doing this. I won't. I have to focus on my career right now."

"Of course—"

"Good-bye." Then he turned and walked away. A steady march. One foot, the other foot. Keep moving. This was his life. He wasn't going to give it up for a piece of ass. No matter how smart, sexy, or fun she was.

...

Tori watched Mike walk away, his body stiff, his hard tones still ringing in her ears. She wasn't a good judge of character by any means. Not because she couldn't put together the pieces, but because she usually didn't care. She didn't want anyone messing around in her emotions, why would she want to do that to anyone else?

But Mike was someone she wanted to understand, so she put her attention to the question of him. Why was he angry? Why had he left?

She recalled every moment of their interaction this morning and focused on his body actions, not his words. He'd been rubbing his shoulder and flexing his fingers. Okay, so that probably meant he'd been in pain. And since men were usually the less rational of the species, she deduced that he'd taken out his pain on the nearest target: her.

Well, that was disappointing, but very human. Plus, she'd done the very same thing to him yesterday when she'd been angry at her sister, so she could hardly throw stones. And on the plus side, he'd left as soon as he'd realized his bad mood so as to minimize the damage. That was very noble of him.

Next question: what was she going to do about it? When Edward was irritable, she would just ignore him. Eventually, he'd find something else to do other than pick at her. Sadly, she'd spent the last year of their relationship waiting for him to get over his problem and stop harassing her. She didn't want to repeat that mistake with Mike. That meant she had to address her neighbor's issue head-on.

What could she do about his damaged shoulder? Short of discovering a mystical healing spell, there really wasn't much.

And though she had a thorough understanding of various magical systems, she sucked at throwing spells. At least the ones she'd tried had never worked. Which left her go-to choice for improving a man's mood. It was a two-pronged attack which began with making him laugh and ended in sex. Either one usually worked, but in combination, it was a sure-fire approach. Assuming, of course, she cared.

That was the biggie. Having finally ditched an unproductive relationship with Edward, did she want to start charming another man just for the hot sex?

Yes. Because it had been really, really hot sex. So good she hadn't even thought it was possible. Which meant she was loath to give it up the morning after discovering it.

Ergo, she was willing to put some effort into charming Mike out of his bad mood. But how?

Stripping naked in front of him wasn't going to work. After all, she'd been naked this morning, and he'd still made a beeline out the door. And since she didn't have any other seduction tricks in her arsenal, she decided to focus on making him laugh.

Well that was easy. Everyone thought it hysterically funny when she proved herself to be clueless. She wouldn't purposely make any mistakes. She detested women who hid their intelligence just to soothe a man, but she didn't have to pretend anything. She was hopelessly out of her depth when it came to renovating her house. She just hadn't cared because she'd decided to have at it anyway. So all she had to do was keep on as she'd been going and not hide her mistakes from Mike.

Easy peezy.

In fact, she'd start right now on her roof.

She was up there within a half hour, making sure to wear tight shorts and an easily stripped away crop top. She tied herself off, even cleared away the debris in her backyard so nothing would trip him up as he ran to her rescue. Then she started hammering.

And she did not make a mistake.

Well, hell. She was pretty damned impressed with herself, even as she was sad that Mike hadn't come around to save her from idiocy.

No problem. There was always that afternoon. Surely he would run out to save her from dehydration or something.

Nope. Which was fine because she had plenty of water. She also had good footing so she never fell off the roof. Not to mention the smarts to rig a pulley system to help her haul those damned tiles up to her roof.

Wasn't she clever? She didn't need any man to come rescue her.

Which ended up depressing her a bit since it would have been lots more fun roofing with someone to talk to. Someone who laughed at her jokes and was sexy as hell with his shirt off. Or on, for that matter.

Damn it. Why hadn't she thanked him for helping her on the roof? Maybe joined him up here yesterday? It certainly would have made the sweltering heat and the constant banging easier to deal with. Not to mention the shared shower they could take as a reward when they were done.

Hell.

For the first time in her life, she really wanted a man to help her accomplish something. Not because she needed it, but because it would be more fun to do it together.

Too bad Mike seemed to have misplaced his hero cape.

Now what?

Chapter Nine

"And do you know what she did yesterday? I swear to God I don't know what to do with her."

Joey narrowed his eyes, his gaze fixed on Mike's arm as they went through some basic shoulder stretches. "Let me guess, she roofed her house."

"No. Well, yes, but she busted her gutters while rigging a pulley system to haul up the roofing tiles."

Joey gently eased Mike's arm down, then slowly pushed it backward to test the resistance. "I thought she was a philosophy professor. 'Ivory tower flake' were your exact words."

"She is."

"Rigging a pulley system doesn't sound—"

"She's smart, okay? That's not the point."

Joey snorted. "Smart, sexy, roofs her own house—"

"And busts the gutters."

"Inexperienced." Joey gestured to Mike to start his regular exercises. "Sounds like a real loser." His tone indicated anything but. "Tell you what, how about during your next barbecue, I mosey over to this gorgeous blonde loser and take her off your hands?"

Mike's right side was aching like the devil, but there was nothing wrong with his left side as he accidentally dropped a barbell on Joey's foot. Well, he tried. Sadly, the man was quick on his feet.

"Tori needs you like she needs a hole in the head."

Joey just chuckled. "Well if you don't want her..."

"I didn't say that!" Except he had. Repeatedly. And he was still waiting for his dick to get the message. "Look, just because I'm not going to date her doesn't mean I want her set up with a jerk like you."

"Hey!"

"Look asshole, you use 'em and lose 'em faster than anyone I know. And considering the guys I know? That puts you deeply in asshole territory."

"I can't help it if there're lots of them who want what only I can give."

Mike looked for another barbell, but there wasn't one close enough to grab. Besides, Joey was right. The women did flock to his dark good looks and I'm-a-jerk air of aloof charm. It made no sense, but basketball bunnies rarely did. His best guess was that they all thought they would be the one to break through to the man's guarded heart. Wasn't going to happen. As far as he could tell, the man only cared about money. Hence his job as personal trainer to the mega-rich. Good thing he was great at it.

"Tori's not for you," Mike said with a grunt as he tried to push his shoulder too far. "Besides, you don't want her. She comes with too much baggage."

Joey passed him a wussy two-pound weight and told him to start lifting it slowly. God, he felt like an idiot.

"What's wrong with her? She got a twisted past? Abusive ex?"

"Idiot ex. He showed up last night at midnight. Leaned on the doorbell like Godzilla was attacking. Fucking moron."

"He woke you?"

"It was my fucking house."

Joey frowned a bit then finally understood. "First off, it's my parents' house. At my suggestion, they're letting you house-sit. And second, the idiot banged on your door not hers?"

Mike dropped the tiny weight and breathed into the ache, letting the shoulder recover a bit before his next set. "He's paying me a hundred bucks to keep an eye on her."

Joey stared at him. "I don't even know where to begin asking questions. A hundred—"

"Yeah, he's a cheap bastard. Tori and I bought beer with it."

"Now there's a good idea."

Then Mike thought back. "No wait. That was the sister's five hundred. I won moron's hundred by kissing Tori."

Joey just grinned. And when Mike turned toward him, the guy gestured with his free hand. "Just keep talking. Clearly I have no idea what's going on."

"He showed me engagement rings."

"Idiot ex?"

"Cheap idiot ex. Wanted to know if I'd been checking up on her and if she'd taken up with anyone."

"You tell him you'd slept with her?"

"How the fuck do you know that?"

Joey started laughing. It was a small chuckle that grew. The more Mike glared at him, the more the man gave in to his humor until he was leaning against the weight rack and wiping his eyes.

"You done yet?" Mike groused.

"Never thought I'd see you this screwed up over a girl. Jesus, how long ago did you sleep with her?"

"None of your damn business."

"I'm guessing about six nights ago. You've been a whiny bitch ever since."

Mike told him succinctly what the man could do with his opinion. Which only set off some more laughter. Asshole.

"Look, the ex is planning on proposing. I told him to go buy a big damned rock and to not darken my doorstep again."

Joey was smiling, but as the silence lengthened, his expression slipped away. "You're serious. The guy is planning on proposing?"

"Yup."

"And you slept with her?"

"Yup," he said, his voice growing softer as he remembered. Damn, it was the best sex of his life, and he'd run away like a scared thirteen-year-old boy. He wasn't proud of how he'd ended it with her, but damn it, this was why he was a star player with the NY Knicks: because he made the hard decisions and stuck with them. "It was a mistake."

"Well it was someone's mistake, we don't know whose yet. So you think she'll say yes?"

The very idea made his gut clench. Tori stuck with Edward for the rest of her life? Talk about marrying a dead fish. And a cheap one, too. But out loud, he repeated what he'd been saying to himself ever since the idiot had showed up at his door. "It's not my problem."

"Right. Because you're not hung up on her at all."

"God, no."

"Course not. Just because she's all you've talked about for two weeks now."

"It hasn't been two weeks," he grumbled. More like twelve and a half days. "And you know why." Mike was sweating as he tried his first exercise again. It was a simple damn thing. Walking his fingers up the wall, but shit…it felt like he was running a marathon one finger at a time.

"You know," Joey said, his tone conversational. "I've listened to every superstition you nutcases can dream up. Lucky shorts, purple socks, three green beans with a steak dinner. I'm sure one of you dances naked and howls at the moon before every game. I'm all for whatever gets you to a winning season, but, Mike, your system is straight up stupid."

"It's not stupid. It's about focus and time. There's only so much—"

"Bullshit."

Mike dropped his arm and glared at Joey. "You don't have to understand it. Just know that it works."

"Fine, it works. You're a monk. But I'm giving you until your next barbecue to get your head out of your ass or I'm moving in."

"What?"

"I've got a thing for smart blondes."

Mike rose to his most intimidating height. "You're un-invited."

"I'll crash it."

"I could pick you up and throw you across the room."

"Not without ripping up your shoulder, you can't."

It was a measure of how insane Mike was that he actually considered it. But after a few furious breaths, he realized the ass was right.

No reason Tori couldn't date Joey if she wanted another jerk in her life. At least he was better than Edward, though only marginally. But first—before either of those losers made their move—he was going to make damn sure she understood what his "friends" were like.

"We done?" he asked, his tone surly.

"Yup. See you tomorrow."

It took him ten minutes to shower, an eon to drive home, and then thirty seconds to get to Tori's house. Though God knew when he found her, she wasn't doing anything he'd envisioned on the way over. She hadn't tumbled off the roof or redesigned her rock garden—again. And she hadn't been baking, as far as he could tell. Nope. She was sitting alone in a dark house holding a flashlight between her teeth as she paged through a book on Mayan architecture.

"Tori?"

She jumped, obviously startled, and the flashlight fell out of her mouth. It dropped with a thud onto the still unfinished floor. "Mike! I didn't hear you come in."

He didn't know how she could have missed him stepping through the back door and calling her name. But then again, his mother used to joke that a nuclear bomb could go off during practice and he wouldn't hear it. That kind of focus was an asset as long as prowlers didn't sneak into your house while you were deep in temple designs.

"What are you doing?" he asked rather than follow his own illogical train of thought.

"I got frustrated."

"With the Mayans?"

"What? Oh! No. I've always been interested in Mayan religious thought, but I'd never looked before at their architectural feats."

He nodded, guessing where her mind had gone. "So all this home improvement has got you thinking about the ancient way of building."

"Not really," she said with a smile. "More about how they lived without electricity."

He looked at the floor behind her and saw the electrical how-to book. He scanned her fingers quickly. No burn marks that he could see, but then again, it was kind of dark in here. "What happened?"

She shrugged. "I broke my electricity."

"How?"

"Well, if I knew that—"

"You'd have already fixed it. Right." He squatted down before her. Her cheeks were rosy from the heat—the air conditioning was out with the electricity—and there was a light sheen of sweat on her face. It occurred to him that his mother would be screaming bloody murder if her electricity went out, even if she'd been the one to break it. His cousins, too, would be bitching about an electrician and cursing their bad luck. None of them would be sitting calmly in a corner and reading a book by flashlight.

"Do you want some help?" he asked, impressed again by her odd, level-headed approach to life.

She sighed, and her eyes dropped down in disappointment. "I've called an electrician. I just don't have the focus to figure it out."

He dropped down beside her on the floor. "It's not a failure to hire a professional." He looked around. "How old is this house anyway? It probably has some tricky wiring."

She sighed. "It's all tricky. Don't tell Edward, okay? He'll just claim I've come to my senses."

He frowned at her. "Why would I tell him?"

"Why would he bang on your door after midnight and stay for a half hour last night?"

"Because he's a moron."

She nodded, clearly accepting his pronouncement. "Did you tell him about us?"

He shifted uncomfortably. "No. Because there is no us. That's what I came to tell you."

She frowned at him. "You already made that clear."

He nodded. "Yeah, but I didn't explain why. I want to now."

What the fuck was he saying? He had no interest in sharing this with her, and yet here he was settling down beside her. And as he stretched out his legs, he realized that this felt right. Talking to her felt really…right.

"Want me to get some beer?" she asked.

He shook his head. "It won't take that long." A quick explanation, a warning about Joey and any of his other so-called friends, and he was out of here.

"Okay."

Then she waited. She set aside the book and folded her hands in her lap. And she waited. While he wondered what exactly had possessed him to start this conversation.

"Um... So back in high school I developed a system. And, um, I had to refine it in college, but it's worked for me. It got me to NBA."

She nodded. "A system. Of behavior."

The word "superstition" echoed annoyingly through his brain, but he ignored it. Instead, he looked out at the locust tree where it overshadowed her backyard and threatened her roof. One bad ice storm and it could crack and break through her newly shingled roof. "It's about proper allocation of resources. About planning for the future and not just letting things happen willy nilly." Like a tree growing to maturity in the wrong place in her yard.

Meanwhile, she stretched out her legs beside him, leaning back in much the same position as they'd been many nights ago. A wonderful, amazing night.

"Bullshit," she said.

He'd been so busy thinking about her legs and what she'd done with them on that night that it took him a moment to process her words. When he did, he twisted to stare at her.

"What?"

"Bullshit," she repeated. "It's about a girl." He opened his mouth to argue, but she kept talking. "You were talking high school and college. It has to be about a girl. Or two girls."

"It could be about a coach. A great coach."

"You said high school *and* college. You didn't have the same coach."

Okay. So she could make intelligent deductions. "Fine. It was about some girls."

She grinned. "Tell me everything."

He chuckled and began to speak.

Chapter Ten

Tori settled in to listen to his tale. She loved story time, and more than that, she was thrilled to learn anything she could about him. She'd already read everything there was on the internet and quite a bit that had been at the library in back issues of *Sports Illustrated*. He was her newest obsession, and she intended to glut herself on all things Mike. But first she had to keep him around. And talking.

"Come on," she prompted. "Who was she?"

"The first girl," he said, his mouth pulled wide into a superior grin, "was my mother."

She nodded, knowing that culturally the African-American mother was a significant force in a young man's life. Certainly more than her own mother had influenced her. His father had been the Caucasian guy who'd skipped soon after he was born, but his stepfather had stuck around. Still, it was clear his mother had been the stabilizing influence. "She raised a fine man."

He smiled, and she could tell he still had a good relationship with his mother. "We weren't dirt poor, which helped a lot. There wasn't the pressure to join the gangs and I showed promise early in basketball. It was the only thing I really loved, and she tied everything to that. I couldn't go shoot hoops unless my homework was done. If I didn't do my chores, she'd drag me out of the playground by my ear."

"Sounds like a fierce woman."

"You have no idea. Once I got it in my head that I was too big for her to spank. I didn't realize she had another weapon."

Tori twisted, her thighs braced against his, the heat of his body thrilling hers. "What did she do?"

"Started telling stories to the guys on the playground. Stories about wearing my sister's ballet stuff." He shuddered. "Some of them still call me Tutu."

She laughed. "Smart woman."

"It wasn't even true, but the more I denied it, the more the name stuck."

"You did your chores after that?"

He nodded. "Never openly defied her again."

She leaned into the wall and her hands brushed his. She liked the feel of his calluses and the way the afternoon light made his skin look warmer—like cocoa after the whipped cream had melted.

"So was the system her idea?"

"Not in so many words. Mom was all about staying the course, as she put it. My father had skipped when I was still in diapers."

"I read that. I'm sorry."

"Mom learned her lesson then. She wanted a man who would stay the course. And she'd be damned if her son grew up to be another here and there, disappearin' man." His voice took on the higher notes of his mother's words. The woman must have said those words a million times.

"I'd love to meet her sometime," she said. "She sounds like quite a woman."

"She is." His expression softened. "I think she'd like you."

Tori laughed to cover the flash of pain at his words. "I doubt it," she said, keeping her voice light even though she was exposing her biggest flaw. "I'm the female version of here and there, disappearin' man."

He frowned. "How many years were you with Edward?"

She waved that away. "That was laziness, not commitment."

His expression shifted to confusion as he studied her face. "You really believe that, don't you? That you're flighty."

She shook her head, uncomfortable with the shift to her own issues. "I live in my own world," she said. "And my passions are many." She waved vaguely at the boxes of books in the other room.

"And yet you've got a PhD, you teach at one of the most prestigious universities in the country, and you're renovating a house all by yourself."

She shrugged. "That means I've learned to manage my obsessions to personal gain." That had nothing to do with her ability to hang with a man over the long haul. It wasn't the man's fault. She usually got bored with him way too fast. Which brought her back to her current obsession. "Back to your mom. I doubt she told you that you couldn't have both a woman and basketball."

He chuckled. "Actually, she did. But only after I had gotten myself into trouble."

She tilted her head close to him. "Are we about to talk about high school?"

He mirrored her movement such that they were almost nose to nose. "We are. But…" He swallowed, clearly nervous. "This story hasn't hit the press. I'd rather it never did."

She blinked, taking a moment to understand what he'd just said. "Did you just warn me away from talking to the press?" she asked. Then before he could answer, she started giggling.

"What?"

"The idea that the press would want to talk to me." She laughed harder. "I mean, I'm rising to the top of my field and only about three people in the world care what I say. You can't possibly think the press—"

"If they knew about you, Tori, knew that we'd been together, they'd be here."

She stopped laughing, but only because she was so absorbed with the unusual idea that reporters would ever want to talk to her. But of course, they didn't care about her. It was about him, and she was fine with that. "Don't worry. The only reason to talk to the press is for either fame or money. I don't want one and have plenty of the other."

He picked up her hand and pressed a kiss to her palm. "You are one unique woman," he said. Then he pulled away, but stayed to trace a finger along the lines of her hand. "I like the fame, Tori."

Of course he did. It was part of being a media darling and a superstar athlete. "Then you should enjoy it. But don't think I care one way or another about it."

"Fair enough."

He was wandering off topic again. And wasn't that a surprise that she noticed when she was the queen of random thoughts? "High school," she prompted.

"I got a girl pregnant."

She winced at both his words and the unexpected stab of jealousy.

"Well," he amended before she could say anything. "I thought I did. Turns out she wasn't, but those were some bad weeks."

"Were you going to keep the child? Marry her?"

"Absolutely. And then five minutes later, absolutely not. I waffled back and forth, thinking I'd quit school and get a job. Then I thought she ought to give up the baby. Then I thought she wouldn't and I would have to find a way to support her and go to college. I could give her my scholarship money..." His free hand waved in the air while his gaze slid away. "It was a mess. I was a mess."

"Which is when your mom invented the system, right?"

He nodded. "It's not like it was a new idea, but she laid it out crystal clear. I had to pick what I wanted to do in life and stick with it. And that meant not getting sidetracked into women, into parties, into...everything else."

"You wanted basketball." Obviously.

"Yeah. But I would have stuck by the girl. I wasn't going to be my father and skip."

Of course not. "But then she turned up not pregnant—"

"And I broke it off. No more girls. No more sex. No more mistakes. I wanted to play pro ball."

"And you did."

He shook his head. "It was never that easy. I had a girlfriend in college, too. She was a lot like you. Smart. Feisty. A German major and hot as hell. I'd learned the lesson about wearing a condom, but not about focus."

"Did she distract you?"

"Got me to try ecstasy. Fucked me up royally, and I fell down a flight of stairs. Sprained my wrist, banged up my head, and taught me a lesson."

"Not to dabble and drive...er, walk?"

"Not to dabble at all. It only takes a single moment with your eye off the ball. One little pill and all my dreams could have disappeared. Poof."

She was silent, absorbing his words. She knew what it took to reach the top of a field. Of course she did. But until this moment, she hadn't really processed that a pro athlete had to be vigilant all the time. It was his body on the line. She could break a leg and still write her papers. He couldn't even experiment in college without risking everything.

She understood pinpoint focus. Hell, she could be as driven as any pro athlete—for a time. But to keep that kind of discipline all his life without wavering? She couldn't even imagine it.

"You're more impressive the more I know you," she said.

"You're the only woman in the world more impressed by my failures than my accomplishments."

She chuckled. "Staying disciplined over the long haul is not a failure. It's a monumental achievement. On the order of the Mayan temples."

"And here I just thought I played really good ball."

She looked at him, her gaze roving over his face, but seeing more than just his features. She saw the movement of his body when he played and the agony of a teenager who thought his entire life was over. She saw a man who'd caught her out of the air at the risk of his shoulder, and also the man who'd run out of her bedroom for a reason she was only beginning to understand.

"I want to sleep with you again," she blurted. "But I don't want to screw with your system."

"Do you want to wait ten years?" he asked. "That's about how long I have until my career's over."

She winced. She often couldn't wait thirty minutes for a pizza. "Not likely," she confessed.

"Yeah. Me either." And then he kissed her. It was a thorough kiss, for all that it was swift. A touch of their mouths, a thrust of his tongue, and a duel that left her breathless before he pulled back.

"Mike?" she asked, startled by how husky the word sounded.

"It's just a temporary thing, right? No commitments."

"I live in the moment, Mike. You know that."

"I don't."

She leaned forward and nipped at his lower lip. "Maybe

you should try."

He grinned. Then he reached up with one hand to stroke her chin. He was searching her eyes for something, she had no idea what. "I came here to tell you that my friends are going to hit on you. That if you get tired of me, there are plenty of other fish—"

"Jesus, like I don't know that," she interrupted.

He blinked, obviously startled.

"I learn from my mistakes. I'm not going to hang around when it's gone wrong. I should have dumped Edward long ago. The minute you start boring me, you're out of here." It was a lie. She already knew she'd put up with a lot of bad to stay with Mike. He understood her. He laughed at her jokes. He let her make her own decisions. And he never once talked down to her. She figured it was more likely he would get tired of her.

Meanwhile, he was laughing. "Fair enough," he said. Then he went back to kissing her. His hand stroked up her cheek and into her hair while the other one began caressing her thigh, teasing along the edge of her cutoffs.

She shivered at his large hands, loving the feel of him touching so much of her and yet needing more. "Can we do it my way this time?" she asked.

His lips curved into a smile. "Can you do it while still making eye contact?"

She frowned for a moment, then realized she'd spoken words aloud. That's how much he distracted her when he touched her. She ended up mouthing words that had little connection to her brain. And yet…she liked that he would let her take control. "Will you let me handcuff you? And have my wicked way with you?"

He snorted. "If you like."

She frowned at him. "You don't seem turned on by the idea."

His expression turned naughty. "Baby, I'm turned on by you. It doesn't matter how. Have at it." Then he touched her chin. "But you give me the key. I won't use it unless you get weird. But I—"

"Deal." She might have argued that having the key wasn't truly surrender, but honestly, she never remembered the safe word anyway. It was better if he kept the key. She trusted that he would play fair.

"Eye contact all the time? No wandering off while I'm cuffed to the bed."

She laughed. "Okay. But you can close your eyes and scream if you want."

"Not going to happen."

"Are you su—ooh!" And once again, she was being hauled to her feet by his good arm. She laughed, thrilled to be lifted so easily. She'd bet anything that once he got his rotator healed, he'd be throwing her over his shoulder caveman style. Which was all kinds of good with her. "The handcuffs are in my desk."

He'd been heading for her bedroom, but stopped. "Which is where…?"

"Oh. Right. Upstairs." She'd converted an upstairs bedroom to her office. She led the way while he kept their hands intertwined. Three steps down the hall and into the room and there it was. Her metal monstrosity of a desk that had once been her grandfather's. It was lime green and was always cool to the touch. She loved it even before he maneuvered her to sit down on the top of it.

"Before we get to the handcuffs," he said, "I want to spend some time kissing you."

She grinned. That worked for her. She gestured to the massive desk chair that went with the massive desk. All metal except for the leather seat. It had armrests that curved down into the frame and would be perfect in just a few minutes. But he didn't know that as he settled onto it and then rolled right up between her legs.

Then it was kissing, teasing, nipping, and generally a wonderful good time. God, why had she never done this before? Why had she always rushed through? Because it had never occurred to her that this could be fun. Or that any man would be patient enough to do this for so long.

Which by her estimation was about ten minutes before she got so hot and bothered that she wanted the main event. Like now.

She broke away from his mouth, her heart pounding hard in her chest, and her bottom slick against the metal. "Top drawer to the right." He grinned at her and pulled open the drawer to reveal all her bills stuffed to bursting. Oops. "To my right," she amended.

He shifted to the other side, pulling it open to reveal random pens, paperclips, and four pairs of handcuffs. Two plastic cheapies, a pink fuzzy one, and one wrapped in black leather.

Mike frowned. "Is this something you do often?"

"Never. Those are all party favors."

He laughed. "You go to different parties than I do."

"Really?" That didn't fit with the wild sports party image she'd had in her brain.

"Really," he said seriously.

She shrugged. "Don't worry. Academics like to pretend they're wild, but for the most part my friends get off on talking about their field of study. Boooorrrring." She reached down and pulled out the pink furry one. "I can't believe I'm going to finally get to try these."

He heaved a sigh, though she could see laughter in his eyes. Not turned on—well not by the handcuffs—but a beautiful sense of fun that lifted the joy in her, too. Was this what it was like to date a man who played games for a living?

She didn't know. She just knew that she was going to play with Mike, and that was beyond thrilling.

Snick.

She'd snapped one cuff onto his wrist. Wow. Even his wrists were big.

"That's not hurting is it?"

"Only my manly appeal. Did you have to use the pink ones?"

She snapped the other side onto the metal armrest. "Quiet, Tutu. I chose this one on purpose."

He grumbled at that nickname, but she just grinned as she grabbed the leather cuffs. But he kept his hand out of her reach. "Not until I get the key. Don't want you wandering off, forgetting that I'm trapped here as your prisoner."

"Hmmm," she said, liking that idea. But she pressed the key in his hand anyway. "You sure you can work it?"

"You'd be surprised what my fingers can do."

And wasn't that a suggestive idea? She lost focus for a moment imagining all the possibilities, but when his free hand slid up between her thighs, she came back to the present real fast. Oh wow. Even one-handed and through the heavy fabric of her cutoffs, he was already stroking her clit to trembling awareness.

"Oh yes," she murmured, her hips working against his hand. "Oh wow."

"Take off your shorts," he said. "Strip them off for me, Tori." Then he stopped what he was doing, and she had to force herself back to lucidity.

"Damn, you're good."

He just grinned.

Snick.

One leather cuff on his free hand. A moment later, she had him latched to the other armrest. She didn't even forget to give him the key.

"Well, hell. Now I won't be able to finish what I started."

She leaned down, making sure her breasts were in full view. "You're supposed to say I'm good, too."

"I don't like stating the obvious."

She grinned and reached down to his shorts. That erection must be hurting given how thick and hard it pressed against the fabric. It took her a few fumbling moments, but she got him undone. His always impressive member pushed into her hand, and she enjoyed giving it some attention. A few strokes, a pinch at the tip, and a wicked lick of her lips while his breath shortened and his nostrils flared.

"Do you like that?" she asked.

"You know I do."

"Yeah," she said. "I know." Then she abruptly used her feet to spin him away from her. He stopped his motion quickly enough. His feet weren't tied down, but she'd accomplished what she intended. He wasn't locking her against the desk anymore. And he was hot and hard and frustrated.

She knew the feeling.

Meanwhile, she hopped off the desk and moved to stand in front of him.

Striptease time.

Well that's what she intended. Except now that it came to it, the idea was better in concept than in execution. She was busy rolling her pelvis around and trying to be seductive with her arms, but it really didn't work. She had no natural sense of rhythm and nothing in her body worked in a coordinated pattern.

"I need music," she said.

"No baby," he said, his voice a low rasp. "You're doing just fine. Take off that tee for me. Just pull it off."

She could do that. In fact, she could do it slowly, one bare inch at a time. Well, at first. About two seconds after her vision was blocked, she lost patience and hauled it off. That left her in a lacy red bra.

Mike grinned and his eyes smoldered. "Nice. Now how about those shorts?"

She could do that, too. She unbuttoned, and then slid the zipper down. Then on sudden inspiration, she spun around and slowly bent over. She was pretty flexible thanks to a regular yoga class, and so she was able to drag the shorts down while lifting her bottom high in the air. The matching lace thong was just a lucky accident. Normally, her underwear was a mismatched jumble of whatever was clean.

Mike's groan was all the encouragement she needed. Apparently he was right. She didn't need music. She peeked at him from around her ankle. She had to maintain eye contact right? What she saw was a sheen of sweat on his forehead and an erection that had swelled impossibly large. Maybe she should help him with that.

"Back up, baby," he said.

"What?"

"Don't straighten up. Just back up. A little more. A little…"

He'd directed her to back up until his hand could reach her. He could have just slid forward on the chair. It was on rollers, but clearly he was staying with the game, pretending to be immobilized.

She heard the clatter as the key dropped to the floor. And while she was looking in surprise at the tiny thing, she felt the very tips of his fingers caress her bottom. He feathered against her, but quickly adjusted. Soon he was slipping beneath her thong, pushing his fingers between her folds before slipping inside. She hadn't intended this. Cuffing him had been about her taking control. But this was…wow. This was amazing.

He pushed his finger into her, and she clenched around him. Her head was spinning—in part from the angle, in part from the feel of him stroking her—and so she grabbed hold of the desk to anchor herself.

"Mike," she gasped. He was right. She was surprised by what he could do with just his fingers. In and out, spreading her folds, then stretching forward to rub her clit. "Oh God."

She felt his lips on her lower back. He was kissing her, nipping her skin while she rode his hand. "That's it baby," he said into her flesh. "Come for me."

He was circling her clit, stroking her faster and faster. But at his words, he pushed against it. A quick stab shot her straight to the moon.

She cried out, arching as she bore down on his hand. He kept pulsing the pressure, up against her over and over while her orgasm crashed through her.

It lasted forever and not long enough. Her knees gave out and she fell away from his reach. It was fine though. She felt wonderful, and he was obviously pleased with himself. She was on the floor now, looking up at his grin. Languor making her legs weak and her gaze soft. And once again, her words tumbled out.

"I was wrong."

"What, baby?"

"I was wrong," she repeated as she slowly stretched her legs out. Mmmmm, she felt amazing. Her head dropped against the desk as she looked at him, all big and stunning even handcuffed to a chair.

"About?"

"I thought I wanted to be in complete control, but…" She shook her head. "It's more fun to play together."

He lifted his arms. "So uncuff me and I'll show you—"

Ding dong.

She looked up. So did he.

"Electrician?" he asked.

She shook her head. "Not until tomorrow."

"Oh. Then—"

Ding dong.

Suddenly she remembered. "Oh shit. It's Wednesday."

"It's Thursday."

"I know. But he's just like me. Can't keep track of time." She snatched up the key, her mind working overtime. If she was right, he'd start banging on the door in about three seconds.

Mike was already working on the leather cuff. "Who is it?"

She couldn't get the damned key past the pink feathers and into the lock. He was moving too much, so she abandoned him to pull on her shorts.

Bang bang bang.

Yup. There he was.

She fumbled zipping up her cutoffs. She glanced at Mike, her sense of the ridiculous making her giggle. At least he'd gotten one cuff off and was now scanning the floor for the other key. She tried to tell him she had it, but it was too late.

She heard the front door open. Oh hell. Only one person had the other key to her house. She grabbed her tee, pulling it down.

"Tori? Honey, are you here?"

She straightened the shirt then fluffed out her hair. "Coming, Daddy!" she called.

Mike's head shot up. "Daddy?" he mouthed.

She nodded, then dashed out the door, nearly tripping as she flew down the stairs. "Hi there!" she called, hugging her father tight.

Then there were the usual pleasantries. The how are you, where's Mom, what's going on type questions. It wasn't until they'd wandered into the kitchen together that she thought to wonder what the hell was taking Mike so long. He couldn't be hiding up there, could he?

So she went to the bottom of the stairs. "Mike?" she

called. "Come on down. I want you to meet my father."
Silence. "Mike?"

"There someone up there?" her father asked, coming to
join her.

"Yeah," she said. "My neighbor. You'll like him."

The two of them climbed the stairs and headed for the
office. Surely he'd had plenty of time to get himself together
by now.

"Mike?" she repeated, then they rounded the corner to
see fully into the office.

Which is when she realized that she still had the key to
the pink fuzzy cuffs in her hand.

Chapter Eleven

Mike had one prayer: *Don't come up here. Don't come up here.* It was her father, for God's sake. And he was sitting handcuffed to her desk chair with his shorts undone. And no matter how he tried, he wasn't going to be able to hide the pink fuzzies.

Never in the history of his dating girls had he ever made a good impression on a father. He was too big and — in his younger years — too wild. For once, he really wanted to show himself to be a decent guy to a dad. Just once.

But in this, his prayers were not answered, and up they came. First Tori's light step, quickly followed by the heavy tread of her father's. Fuck. He tried one last time to button his fly and failed again. At least he wasn't bursting out of it anymore. Nothing like having the girl's father walk in to cause massive shrinkage.

One last useless jerk of his arm — the damn chair was made out of steel — and then they were there. He tried to twist so the cuffs weren't in view. It didn't matter as Tori blushed an adorable pink and held up the key.

"I'm so sorry, Mike. I completely forgot."

Yeah. He'd figured that out.

Meanwhile, he looked to the middle-aged father. Stocky build, about four hairs left on his balding pate, and a laser focus behind heavy, dark glasses. And naturally, he was looking straight at the pink cuffs. Great.

"Dad, I'd like you to meet Tutu."

"Tori!" Mike groaned.

"Well, I have to explain the cuffs somehow. He was letting me try them out. I wanted to see if they pinched on a man his size."

Jesus. He supposed Tutu was better than his real name. Just what the tabloids needed: a story about him in pink handcuffs.

Mr. Williams stepped forward. "Pleased to meet you, son." He reached out to shake Mike's right hand, but that was the one currently being restrained. Mike adjusted, offering up his left hand but that never worked with anyone.

Then there was the excruciating tick-tock of time passing as Tori fumbled with the cuffs. He hadn't been so embarrassed since being caught in middle school behind the bleachers with Lizzy Cantor.

Fortunately Tori was more than able to fill the silence.

"So is Mom still gone?"

"Not still. Again." Her father rocked back on his heels, shoving his hands in his pockets just as if this was the most normal thing in the world. "Just dropped her off at O'Hare then came over here."

Tori glanced at Mike. "It's our Wednesday lunch."

Except it was Thursday dinner.

Snick.

The cuffs dropped off him, thank God. Then a quick button of his fly and he could stand up and meet Tori's father like a man. Maybe he could salvage the experience. Except he was significantly taller than Mr. Williams. He towered over most men, but Mr. Williams was more on the diminutive side. Which meant he tried to stay in a half crouch as he extended his hand, but the man was tilting backward as he looked into Mike's eyes.

"I thought point guards were short."

Shit. The man recognized him. He'd gotten so used to Tori's family and friends being clueless that he was momentarily startled by the awareness in the guy's eyes. Not starstruck, though. Just not clueless.

"Um, we are," he finally said. "Relatively speaking."

The man's eyes went to Mike's hurt shoulder. "So are you out?"

"Not yet, I'm not."

Mr. Williams nodded. "Good. Not a fun game if the Bulls just trounce you." Then he glanced at his daughter. "Your mom's got me in the mood for some sushi. And peach pie." Then he looked back at Mike. "What about you, Mr. Giamaria?"

"Please, call me Mike."

"It's probably better than Tutu."

"Yes. Much." Then he hesitated. He didn't want to step on father/daughter time. "Tori, I can eat a lot of sushi, and you probably want to be alone—"

"Oh good. You like sushi, then."

"I love it, but that doesn't mean—"

She cocked her head at him. "Really, Mike. If you're worried about how much you're going to eat, you can pay." She looked at her father. "Agreed?"

Her dad shrugged. "I'll get the peach pie, then."

She grinned. "Deal!" Then she linked arms with both men and began leading them out of the room. Well, she linked arms with her father, and then held Mike's hand. There wasn't room on the stairway for all three of them to walk side by side.

They ended up taking Mike's car. No way was he going to fit comfortably in her little Prius or her father's orange VW bug with "Sunkissed" painted on the side. Tori had apparently written it in magic marker years ago, and her father loved it so much he'd had it professionally painted.

Which became part and parcel for how the evening went. On the one hand it was like having dinner with Odd and Odder. Conversation wandered eclectically from highway construction through an art exhibit to stock prices and African rainfall. The connections those two drew between the most disparate things boggled his mind and yet was incredibly stimulating. When her father started comparing basketball plays to a termite invasion, Mike really got into the spirit of things.

He loved the way Tori's mind worked, and with her father he could see just where she got it from. And though he had the distinct impression that they each had more than double his IQ points, he never felt left out. Confused, every now and then, but not left out. In short he had a great time.

Until the paparazzi showed up.

He thought he'd managed to hide from them. Plus, it wasn't during the season, so unless he was dressing up as a catholic school girl or something—like wearing pink handcuffs—then no one should have cared where he was or what he was doing.

Except there was always a hungry reporter looking for fodder for the gossip rags. And whereas he would just ignore it, neither Tori nor her father were used to this type of attention.

He'd spotted the man early. The stooped guy in a hoodie had come into the quiet restaurant, sat at the sushi bar and snapped a few pictures. Mike leaned back, choosing to give the man a good picture of him eating sushi—really groundbreaking photojournalism there—before turning his back on him. Besides, they were having a fascinating conversation about the samurai code as it ought to apply to professional athletes.

Which is when Tori pulled a Sharpie out of her purse. She grabbed her paper placemat and flipped it over to write something in thick black letters. He couldn't see what and before he could ask, she flashed him a mischievous smile.

"Will you kiss me in public?"

He hesitated. Did he want to declare his relationship with her publicly? Sure. After all, he'd been photographed with scores of women. Unless he said any different, she would be just another one in the crowd as far as the papers were concerned. But was she remotely prepared for the attention it might garner her?

"You sure?"

She grinned. "Yeah. I'm sure."

"Okay."

So he leaned forward. He knew that he was giving the reporter a good shot. In fact, now that he thought about it, there weren't pictures of him kissing anyone except his mother. This would be a first.

She met him halfway, her lips were soft and tasted of the saki she'd been drinking. Lord, she kissed like a dream, especially when she opened so sweetly to the stroke of his tongue. He felt her sigh in delight and could have lost himself in the texture of her. But he was in a public restaurant with her father and a journalist watching. It was time to dial it back.

So he pulled away and picked up his chopsticks, grateful that there was no view of his groin. Though it might be a while before he chanced standing up.

Meanwhile, she set down the paper mat and he finally got a look at what it said.

We need more press about people getting sick from bad water. Just a thought.

www.wateraid.org

He burst out laughing. Okay, so maybe she did have an idea of how to handle the paparazzi. He was so pleased that he could have kissed her again. He could have done a lot more, but once again, her father was sitting there.

Then just when he thought it couldn't get any better, the proprietor of the restaurant showed up with a bakery peach pie. Mr. Williams handed the man two twenties and a few minutes later, Mike was taking huge forkfuls of the best peach pie he'd ever had.

He didn't even have to ask the question. Tori held up her own gooey fork. "We come here a lot and usually call ahead. Mr. Harada knows to keep a peach pie ready for us."

Her father grinned over at him. "Blueberry in the winter."

"And chocolate on my birthday," Tori added.

"Got it. Peach in the summer, blueberry in the winter, and chocolate in May."

Tori blinked. Bet she hadn't realized he knew her birthday. But he'd seen it on her driver's license in her open wallet on the counter. A moment later, she grinned at him.

"A whole month?"

"Why not?"

She seemed to think about it and then agreed. Her father, too, and the conversation continued. Eventually, though, he had to pay the bill and soon they were back at Tori's house.

All in all, it had been a great evening, and he decided he'd done well despite the crappy beginning. At least that's what he thought until they made it to Tori's front stoop when her father cleverly got rid of his daughter.

"Honey, do you mind getting me that book on Egyptian cat motifs you mentioned the other day?"

Tori frowned at him. "Which one? I have dozens."

"Just pick the one you think I'll like best."

"But—"

"I trust you."

She frowned at him, but in the end, she went inside. Mike watched her go, his mind on the fact that she'd obviously *not* locked her front door when they'd left earlier. And then Mr. Williams turned to him.

"That'll keep her busy for a while."

He turned back. "Sir?"

"Look, I know you're neighbors and all, but I just have one thing to say to you."

The man stopped speaking, and Mike was left with a question and a creeping sense of dread in his stomach. In the end, he had to ask. "Sir? What did you want to say?"

Mr. Williams pulled his attention back from an annoying moth that was drawn to the front porch light and focused back on him. "I like watching you play."

"Oh. Thank you."

"But if you hurt my daughter, I'll send the picture to the internet."

"What picture?" Though of course, he already knew.

"Oh. Right." He pulled out his phone and thumbed it on. Two excruciating minutes passed as the man worked to find the picture and then finally passed it to Mike. And there he was, pink handcuffs and all, as Tori was busy unlocking them.

As pictures went, it wasn't that damaging, though his teammates would have a grand time ribbing him about it. The angle didn't show his unbuttoned shorts, and since he had on his shirt, there was nothing scandalous there by today's standards.

What startled Mike was something else in the picture. It was the look on his face as he was watching Tori. She was bent over, clearly fitting key to cuff, so she couldn't have seen it. But the camera did. As had Tori's father.

Mike looked totally enthralled. Infatuated. Besotted. Pussy whipped.

All those words filtered through his mind, not to mention a few more graphic terms that were less than complimentary. He knew he wasn't being led around by his dick. Truthfully, Tori was too distractible to be manipulative. But the look on his face scared him.

That was the look of a man whose world centered around a woman. Not his career, not basketball, not even the normal ebb and flow of life. He had the look of a man in far too deep with a woman, and it terrified him.

He pushed the phone away, panic beating tightly in his throat. "I have no intention of hurting your daughter, sir," he said, barely keeping himself from running back to his house. Not the one next to Tori, but his condo in New York. Jesus, he'd only known her a couple weeks. How the hell had he gotten in so deep so fast?

"Good to know."

Mike waited a moment—a couple heartbeats out of politeness—to see if the man wanted to say anything else. Then he just shook his head. "I think I'm going to call it a night. Got therapy early in the morning."

Her father tilted his head. "You're seeing a psychiatrist? You probably shouldn't say that too loud. Not with reporters—"

"*Physical* therapy," Mike ground out. "For my shoulder."

Mr. Williams blinked then flushed. "Oh, right. Sorry."

Jesus, the whole lot of them were bat-shit crazy. Meanwhile, Tori came back, her arms filled with five different tomes. She could barely see over the stack.

"Dad, I really don't know which one—"

"This one is great, honey," the man answered, pulling the smallest one off the top. "Thanks." Then he leaned down and gave her a kiss. "I gotta get home. You know how your mother worries when I'm gone."

"Dad, you just dropped her off at O'Hare, remember?

She's not home."

"She knows anyway. I'm not sure how, but she knows when I'm out late. And when I don't remember my pills."

"You never remember your pills."

"Exactly."

Then he turned and shook Mike's hand in a firm grip just as if he hadn't just threatened him with internet exposure. "Great meeting you, son. Be careful with that shoulder. Lots of people like watching you play."

"I will—"

"Good night," he said, then he turned around and meandered back to his orange of a car. Mike watched him go, trying to settle the roiling emotions inside him. Damn it, he liked the guy. And he liked the man's daughter. But he couldn't be the Mike in that picture. He couldn't be that out of control.

And so he turned to Tori, meaning to tell her—again—that they were done. But she beat him to the punch.

"You can't spend the night, Mike."

Again with the sucker punch to the gut. "What?"

"I'm still weirded out by my dad seeing you in handcuffs."

"You took the key with you."

"I know. It was totally my fault. But I can't shake the image of Dad standing right there with you...well, you know."

Yeah. He knew.

"I'll have forgotten it by tomorrow, but for tonight..." She gave a shudder. "Besides, I have to draw up some plans for my rock garden."

He looked over at the collection of stones by the side of the house. Sometime in the last few days they'd changed positions and had added two medium-sized orange ones.

"Um..."

"It's a work in progress."

Certifiable. They were all nuts. "Yeah, okay, Tori. I wanted to spend the night alone anyway."

If he expected her to feel hurt by that, he was sorely disappointed. She cocked her head to one side, her blond hair slipping down her shoulder, and she gave him a dazzling smile. Enough that he was momentarily distracted until her words hit him.

"Well, that's good then. We're each on our own tonight."

Was it? Was it good? His brain said yes; his body definitely did not. But it was too late. She stretched up on her toes, gave him a swift kiss on his chin since she couldn't quite reach his mouth, then spun around and bounded back into her house. And while he stood there, he was both pleased and annoyed to hear the snick of the lock. Sure, she'd finally remembered to bolt the door. But he was outside with only the vague scent of ponzu sauce and lemon to keep him company. That and a burning desire to punch something.

"Bat-shit crazy," he muttered as he stomped over to his house. "Totally, completely bat-shit crazy."

Of course, he had no idea if he was talking about them or himself.

Chapter Twelve

Tori shut her front door and immediately let her too bright smile fade from her face.

WTF was she supposed to do now?

She'd seen the look of panic on Mike's face. She had no idea what her father said to him, but it was clear the big bad basketball star was freaking out about something.

Jesus, why did men have to be so touchy?

Normally, she'd just ignore it. That had been her modus operandi with Edward. If he got in a snit, she would just make herself scarce until he figured it out. Which is why she'd made up some excuse and shut the door on Mike.

She was done with waiting for a man to get his act together, right? Which meant she either had to have it out with Mike or wash her hands of him altogether.

Shit, she could kill her father for showing up right then. She'd been all set for a night of hot sex and sweet snuggling when dear, dopey pater had to ruin it.

She dropped her head back against the doorway and let herself slide to the floor. But once there, she noticed all the dirt in the hallway and the paint she wanted to change. She had a busy life right now. An entire house to renovate before fall.

And yet, what she really wanted to do was spend every summer hour she had with Mike. She'd already watched every one of his games on YouTube. He was poetry in motion on the court, and she'd taken the time to learn some of the team's favorite plays. Basketball was a complicated game when it came to measuring one play against another offense. It had been too much for her to process in the short time she'd had, but she was learning quickly.

And right there should be a warning sign to her. When had she ever buried herself in research of a man? Jesus…did that mean…? Could she…?

She couldn't even think the word. After all, she'd thought she was in love with Edward but years later, she could barely think of the man without a sneer. Her other male companions didn't even rank that high. In high school, the boys were too immature for her, and she was too bookish for them. And her college partners were simply sexual explorations that left her cold.

Which meant Mike was in a class all by himself. But was that lo—? Oy. She couldn't think it. To feel that way about a man who was terrified by her father made no sense whatsoever. And yet, she couldn't deny the deep yearning inside. Even now, she was a half breath away from running over to his house. She didn't really want to talk about his panic—or hers—but she wanted to hang out with him. She wanted to drink beer with him. She wanted what came after the beer, too.

So this was lust, she told herself, even though what she felt was so much deeper, so much scarier than lust.

"I need to go to bed," she said loudly. As if the echoing sounds would reinforce the need.

Maybe it did because she stood up and headed for her bedroom. Ten minutes later, she was stretched out on her mattress watching that YouTube video of a slo-mo Mike as he dunked a basket. Shirtless. Powerful. Wonderful.

She was in love.

Damn it.

•••

Mike was going through his nightly shoulder stretches when his phone rang. He wasn't going to answer it. He was too busy stewing about the evening and that damned picture when his shoulder twinged. Shit. He was pushing it too hard.

The phone kept ringing so he reached out and grabbed it even though he knew in his heart exactly who it was. And maybe that was why he was answering because maybe she'd tried to rewire her microwave or something.

"Hello?"

"Hi Mike. It's me."

"Everything okay?"

Long pause that had him straightening up in alarm.

"Tori?"

"I'm sorry about whatever my dad said."

He stifled his groan as he flopped down on the couch. "Your dad is fine. Don't worry about it. I'm not."

"Liar. I saw your face. You're back on that whole system thing again."

Shit. He wasn't used to being with perceptive women. "I told you we're—"

"I'm the one who wanted a rebound lover, remember? How many times do I have to tell you that I'm not going to tie you down? I'm not going to screw with whatever's going on in your head."

He looked up at the ceiling. How did he tell her she was

already screwing with his head? "Tori, it's late. I thought you wanted to just go to bed."

"I lied. I wanted to give you space."

He couldn't help the smile that curved his lips. He'd thought he wanted space, too. But the sound of her voice brought an excruciating awareness of how much he wanted to be with her. Damn it, he didn't want to long for her. That was so high school.

"Do you want me to hang up?" she asked, her voice small.

Yes. No. Hell. "What are you wearing right now?" And where the hell had that question come from? He glared down at his thickening dick. Duh.

"I'm...well, do you want the truth or do you want me to make up some black lace teddy thing?"

Jesus. The image of her in see-through lace had him lurching upward on the couch. He forced himself back down and then...and then...he slipped his nylon shorts down and gripped himself.

"Is it okay if I answer both?"

"Black lace then?"

"Ever had phone sex, Tori?"

"Um...I can't remember."

He blinked. "Really? How could you not remember?"

"This is me. If it wasn't memorable..."

"I got it. You challenging me?"

"I'm..." He could just imagine her now with that look on her face. Part deviltry, part preoccupation. Her head would be cocked to the side while she bit her lower lip and looked up to the right. Thinking. Thinking. "Can I hear you come?"

He nearly choked. "W-what?"

"I'm usually so distracted when you come. I want to hear it. Please?"

She was full of surprises. And apparently, he was more than ready to fulfill her wish. "Um, only if I get to hear you."

He heard her tsk and imagined her full lips pursed in a pout. "You get to hear me—"

"I won't play if you don't."

Pause.

"Okay, but you first."

He was already halfway there, picturing her in a black teddy, her tight ass perked up high enough for him to slip in behind. God he would palm her globes, kneading them as he spread her open.

Then her voice came over the line, husky as she spoke in a raw whisper. "Do you know what I was going to do to you earlier? With you handcuffed in my chair?"

He was pumping his hand slowly, taking his time picturing her bent over and open. All he had to do to touch her breasts would be to lean down and take them. He'd pinch her nipples while her backside writhed over him. He'd push slowly inside.

"I was going to go down on my knees before you. First I was going to lick your fingers—the ones that had touched me—while my hands pulled you out of your shorts. You're so big that I need both hands. I love the way it looks—thick and dark—while my fingers spread over and around."

Jesus. Now he had two fantasies competing in his brain. Her bent over while he pumped into her, and this new one. This awesome one of her on her knees before him. White hands, dark dick.

"Would you lick me?" he rasped.

"Not at first. I want to taste your tip. The salt and the wet. And I read about this thing to do with my hands. It's a rhythmic squeeze of the fingers down the shaft. It feels like a roll, but I've still got hold of everything."

God, he wanted her to do that to him. He wanted to feel all of it. His hand right now wasn't enough to really get it right. It wasn't her.

"First I'd roll my fingers, then I squeeze tight and push

toward the base. It stretches you, you know? And I get to see you push through. I bet I can feel your heartbeat through my fingers."

His hips were working hard now. He couldn't stop it, not with the image of her working his dick, her breasts bobbing into his hands because in his mind he was fondling them. Her breasts. Her hips. Her anything he could touch.

"Lick it, Tori. Tell me how you take me in your mouth."

"I told you. I'll lick the tip, like it's the very top of an ice cream cone. But then I slide my hands lower to stretch you. Then I'll nibble along the ridge. Which do you like best, Mike? Which—"

"All of it, Tori. Take all of me."

"I would. That's the last part. When you're thrusting hard into my hands. When your belly's tight and I can hear your breath loud and harsh. Just like you are now."

He was. Jesus, his heart was pounding. God, he wanted her here.

"Then I open my mouth wide and let you push all the way deep inside. So much you bump against the back of my throat while my tongue strokes you. Guess what happens next."

"What!" It was a demand.

"I suck. Hard. Right now, Mike. I'm sucking you as hard as I can, as deep as—"

He came. He came hard and hot and he must have made noises into the phone, but he didn't even know what they were. It was the hottest thing he'd ever done and he couldn't believe she hadn't been touching him for real.

"God, Tori…" he finally breathed.

"I'm going to hear that in my sleep. That was great, Mike. Thank you."

She was thanking him? Jesus. "Sweetheart, we're not done yet. Let me hear you." Then he smiled. "Or better yet, let me come over and see you."

Silence. Then, "Mike, remember when you asked me what I was wearing and I didn't tell you the truth?"

"Tell it to me now. What are you wearing?"

"Nothing. No electricity, remember? That means no air conditioning."

"Tori, it's like a hundred degrees out there."

"Eighty-four and humid."

She must be sweltering. "Want to come over? In the interest of avoiding heat stroke?"

"Want to shower with me? I'm kinda sticky."

God yes. "You're not getting off that easy. I want to watch you bring yourself off in my shower." Then he was going to spread her legs and do her from behind just like he fantasized. And again front-wise. And again. And again. Until he ran out of fantasies or died of bliss.

"You're not too freaked out?"

He was still freaked out, but other things were taking precedence. "The way I see it, I just need to work through the lust now. Before the season. That way I won't screw with the system."

She didn't answer at first. Lord save him from women who thought instead of just ran over when he invited them to his bed. But even as he waited, he pictured the tips of her white teeth showing as she bit into her bottom lip. Then she spoke.

"I just gotta find my shoes. Oh screw it, I'm coming over barefoot."

"I'm unlocking the door."

"And turn on the shower."

"Nuh-uh. Bathtub."

Pause. "Okay."

What a woman.

• • •

Tori was Sated. Capital S. Totally Satisfied. Totally in love. And totally unwilling to tell him that particular secret. If Mike freaked at meeting her father, the L word would create a nuclear meltdown.

She stretched in his bed, relishing the slide of silk against her sore body. She wondered if these were Mike's or the Ketchums' sheets. Either way, she vowed to buy a set as soon as she could find them on the internet.

She stretched a hand out, feeling the depression that had been filled by Mike. Damn, he was skillful in bed. And in the bathtub. And in the front hallway. He'd made her come right there at the base of the stairs before he'd even let her upstairs to the bathtub.

But now he was gone — off to physical therapy — while she waited with an anxious knot in her stomach to see if he was going to come back with another excuse to keep them apart.

So she lingered there even though he'd told her it would take a couple hours. And just when she was reveling in her memories, the phone rang. She made an effort to keep it with her when her mom was out of town. Just in case.

She answered it badly, cursing as she fumbled to find it. Then she cursed again when she realized who it was. The electrician was waiting for her on her doorstep. So she dressed and went back to her real life. Mike would find her when he came home or he wouldn't. Damn it, she didn't want to care as much as she did, but that was love for you. A complete pain. And a complete wonder.

Maybe she'd spend the afternoon re-reading Aphrodite myths. All in all, the Greeks had it right when they called her a spiteful bitch of a love goddess.

And maybe she'd make Mike come to her for once.

Chapter Thirteen

Tori made a decision that morning. While the electrician set about restoring her power, she resolved to not be an obsessing, clinging woman. It didn't matter what Mike felt or did. The point was that she had some self-respect. She would not throw herself at a man. Especially since he was heading off to the other side of the country in just a few weeks.

So when the electrician left with two weeks' of her pay in his pocket, she decided to bury herself in the pounding beat of African drum music. Now that her air conditioning was restored, she could finish laying down her wood floor. Her decision came right after she spilled coffee—again—on the unfinished sub-floor. It would be healthy hard work, excellent at taking her mind off a man. So she got down on her hands and knees and set about making steady, clear progress.

It almost worked. Every five minutes or so, she would glance at her phone, wondering if he'd called. And when he hadn't, she'd look outside to see if he'd returned home. She couldn't see that from her living room floor, so she'd invent an excuse to wander into the kitchen. Glass of water. Wash her hands. Grab a yogurt. She did them all while looking out the window to his driveway.

Idiot.

So much for her resolve not to be obsessed with him. She'd never been this anxious about a man in her life, and the last thing Mike wanted was another fangirl hanging around. She would not be a clinging woman. It was humiliating. Which sent her back to her flooring until the next time she invented a reason to wander to the window.

Pathetic.

But undeniable.

She'd turned into an obsessed woman.

She sighed and banged the floor with special flair. She was busy tapping out her own drum rhythm in counterpoint to the music when he showed up. She pretended she wasn't hyper-aware of the screen door opening. She pretended to not notice when he leaned against the wall and watched her half dancing, half banging to the music. But when he stayed there, just staring, she finally admitted that she sucked at pretending and looked up at him.

"Don't stop on my account," he said, a sexy grin on his face.

She pushed to her feet then turned down the music. The drums still throbbed through the speakers, but not at a deafening level.

"How was therapy?"

"I told Joey he was not to make any moves on you at the barbecue."

"Is he a jerk?"

"Major."

"Then let him hit on me. I'll shoot him down and you can laugh at him afterward."

His grin widened. "I should have thought of that, but it's too late. I've already staked my claim on you."

She arched a brow. "So you're the only NBA player who

gets to be with me?"

"Sorry," he said as he sauntered away from the door, easily filling her living room with his very hot presence. "I'm afraid the list of people who can't have you is a great deal larger than just the NBA."

"Goodness. You are staking a claim."

He nodded, his large hands going to encircle her waist. "If I'm going to be a rebound lover, then I've got to do it right."

"Right how?"

"Neanderthal how. Me big man, you little woman, that's how."

She arched her brow. "So you're building in the breakup from the start. Because you know I'm not going to tolerate that for long."

His expression sobered. "How long, do you think?"

"Until the sex starts to suck."

He gave a slow nod as he pretended to think about her statement. "I've got to be back on the East Coast at the end of August."

Her heart lurched in her chest, but she did her best to hide it. "Classes start revving up then too." Then she arched her brow, attempting to look saucy. "Think you can keep being spectacular in bed until then?"

"I'm spectacular all year round. In bed or otherwise."

"Wow. That's cocky."

"You have no idea," he said with a chuckle. Then he tugged her steadily closer until her pelvis pressed against his erection.

"Hmmm," she murmured, hating how easily she melted into his arms. "I begin to see your point."

He leaned down. "So long as you feel it, too." He kissed her. Hard and deep. God, she was already keyed up. Her belly was quivering, her breath was short, and she was all but climbing his thighs.

This was not good. Mike would hate a clinging woman, and even if he didn't, she would hate herself. Their relationship was short term, so she had to force some distance between them. She broke the kiss and managed to put all of two inches between them.

"I promised myself I would finish this today," she said, gesturing to the half-done floor.

He nodded, though there was a flash of disappointment on his face. "So do you need any help?"

She smiled. "Need? No, I can handle it myself, but it's more fun with a friend. Assuming your shoulder can take it."

He grinned, rolling his shoulder. "It's healing well. Faster than expected, really, so yeah. I'd be happy to help."

She almost said something about a reward afterward, but held back. She didn't want to bribe him to be with her. And just because she was lusting for his astounding bedroom skills didn't mean she had to admit to it.

She swallowed her words—and her lust—and offered him a mallet. He took it and looked around the floor. "If we finish in an hour, I'll spring for the pizza."

"And I promise to rub your shoulder if it gets sore."

He grinned. "It'll definitely get sore."

She rolled her eyes, but inside all of her went liquid with hunger. But she was not going to be a desperate woman, so she turned away and knelt down to start working. He did the same, but from the opposite side of the row which put him too far away from her, as far as her hormones were concerned.

She ignored them.

And they began to work. Steady banging punctuated by the occasional comment or lemonade break. She kept an eye out to see if he rubbed his shoulder, but there didn't seem to be any hesitation or hitch when he used it. And—to her shame—he caught her looking and did a little elbow dance to the music just to prove that it was solid.

"I doubt that's an approved exercise," she drawled.

"Hmmm. How can I convince you not to tell on me?"

God, they were getting into sexual banter. As if she needed any more reason to watch his biceps flex as he hammered or his thighs bunch as they braced him on all fours. And shit, he was covering twice the area that she was because she was spending so much time ogling him.

She dropped her head and began to work in earnest. She had a damned PhD. She knew how to concentrate when she had to! Except he was really sexy there pounding boards into her floor. And she could really use a break. And what red-blooded woman wouldn't stop to watch?

"We're never going to make that pizza."

"I'm not that hungry anyway."

He looked back. "Really?"

Well, not hungry for food, obviously. And he knew it. "Mike…" she began.

He shook his head. "You set a goal. We finish this floor. Then I'm going to show you what I want way more than pizza."

Okay. So that was a goal she could get on board with. So she picked up her hammer and went to work. Funny what the right incentive could do. They had it done in just over an hour. She hammered in the last board and sat back on her haunches.

"Done," she breathed, beyond satisfied with the work. It looked great and she'd managed to not get distracted by… Ooooo. She felt his hands on her shoulders, big fingers kneading into the knots there. He knew just what she wanted, and her muscles stretched beneath his touch.

"That's good," she breathed.

She felt him lean down until his breath was by her ear. "I have a fantasy, Tori," he said.

She felt her insides quicken. "Isn't that what rebound lovers are for?"

"Will you stay there? On the floor?"

Given what he was doing to her back and shoulders, she would stay wherever he put her. Damn, who knew she'd been so tense? Flooring was hard work. "I'm putty in your hands."

His lips curved against her ear and his breath heated her already flushed skin. Then his hands slid lower on her back. His fingers still pushed into her muscles, but in a few short moments, he'd slid under her shirt before gently pulling it off. Her bra came next, and soon she was sitting there topless.

He kissed along her neck, his hands skimming over her belly. But then he slid up to her breasts, holding them in his large palms. Her nipples were already tight, so he had no problem taking hold of them with two fingers while still palming the rest of her.

Twist, pinch. Squeeze. Pull.

She let her head drop back onto his chest. Her breath deepened while her body liquefied. She reached behind her to touch him, but he nipped at her ear.

"Lean forward, Tori. Onto your hands and knees."

She did with him supporting her as she settled. His fingers slipped to her Lycra shorts, peeling them down with ease. She was shaking with desire as her panties slid down to her knees. Then he supported her while he lifted first one leg then the other to get her totally naked.

There she was, quivering on all fours while he stroked her back, her breasts, and down between her legs. His fingers were long and clever as they pushed through her folds. He was leaning over her, surrounding her as his hand worked between her legs.

"Mike," she gasped, her body struggling to stay still as he worked first deep inside her, then up to her clit.

"Are you ready for me?" he asked.

"God, yes."

He pulled away. She didn't have to look to know that he was stripping out of his clothes and suiting up with a condom.

She heard it clearly even over the music. And better yet, she twisted just enough to see him outlined in sunlight. Taut, passionate man in his prime. Muscles stark, belly rippling with his movements, and a long thick organ stretching for her.

She'd never seen anything more stunningly primal. And she wanted to be mated with him as surely as if she were a cavewoman in need of superior children. Because he was clearly a superior man.

She wet her lips and wanted to say something. But there were no words, only desire. And when he turned back to her, his fingers slipping between her legs, she was arching to meet him in every way she could.

"Are you still ready, Tori?"

She nodded.

Then he crouched down over her. All fours surrounding her. He nudged her legs apart with his knees and thrust into her. Not far. Just the tip, so she moved to him. She spread herself and angled her pelvis for the deepest penetration possible. And she waited.

And waited.

And…

Yes.

He pushed in steadily. Slowly. He was always large, but this seemed to stretch her more than usual. His penetration was like being split apart. And with the drum beats in the background, she felt a pounding in her mind and body—a thrumming that gloried in this possession. And soon he was fully seated.

And still.

He just stopped there. Deep inside her, splitting her wide without moving more. And while she panted from the possession, he began to stroke her. First her arms and her shoulders. He pulled her hair to the side and pressed kisses into her neck and back. Then his hands found her breasts again. Everything he did inflamed her more. And everything he touched sizzled beneath his stroke.

His hands slid to her hips. He gripped her there, lifting her up high enough for him to move. Small pulses of movement at first. A tiny withdrawal, a thick push.

She wanted to squirm, wanted to take him deeper, but he didn't let her. He held her hips just where he wanted, and he took his time.

Further withdrawal, harder thrust.

Again.

Again.

She could hear his ragged breath, and knew he would soon piston in earnest. The impact was growing harder, the movement longer. Better.

"Touch yourself, Tori," he gasped.

She hadn't the focus to do it, but he had such a grip on her mind and body that she couldn't disobey. Less than an hour ago, she'd resolved to be a modern, independent woman. She would not bow to any man's whims. But here she was, spread wide, possessed, and touching herself because he wanted it.

She reached down between her legs, but she didn't find herself. She found him, thick and hard as he slid in and out of her. Hot. Wet. She stretched even further back and found his sack.

He slammed into her and held. She lifted his sac and squeezed. He groaned, the sound muffled against her skin. And when she did it again, he bit her shoulder hard enough to make her body shudder. Sharp pain up high, thick invasion below, and the feel of him around her, both supporting and caging her.

"Now, Tori," he said as he pushed her more fully forward. She had to support herself on one hand because he guided her other to her clit. "Rub yourself."

She pressed hard onto her throbbing bundle of nerves, but she didn't stroke. She was too busy feeling his hands grip her hip bones, adjusting her to the right angle. And then—at last—he began to pound into her.

Hot and hard.

And with each movement, her finger was driven against her clit.

Bam.

Bam.

Her belly tightened. Her breath caught. She wanted to move, but he held her still as he worked in and out of her.

Again.

Again.

Oh God. She couldn't even say the word aloud.

Oh…

Oh…

Detonation.

Her body convulsed, her insides gripped him over and over, and while she was crying out in pleasure, he slammed into her one last time.

Yes!

Release. Or possession. Either one didn't matter.

She loved it, and she loved him.

So when he finally collapsed forward, his belly to her back, she put strength into her arms. She could hold him up, though she didn't need to. Instead, he wrapped his arms around her, he pressed his lips to her back, and then he toppled them over.

Soon she was lying on her back on top of him. He was still inside her and she was stretched out as if flying.

"I'm going to touch you again," he said. "Just as soon as I catch my breath."

"Mike—"

"Shhh…" He lifted his knees, forcing her legs to the outside such that she was spread open again. "Just relax and enjoy the ride. Remember, this is my fantasy. You're doing me a favor."

"Okay," she whispered.

She closed her eyes and surrendered everything to him.

Chapter Fourteen

Mike was going to blow off his morning run and linger in bed with Tori, but she'd kicked him out with the words: "Go on. You're hot when you're sweaty."

It took a minute to figure out what she meant by that. It was early in the morning and he wasn't fully awake. Neither was she, he realized, since she'd burrowed back under the covers. Two minutes later, she was snoring. His woman was not a morning person.

He waited to be freaked out by that thought. Tori as his woman. But the panic didn't come. She wasn't putting any pressure on him. She knew he was going back to New York in a little over a month. Though it stung that she was happy to let him go, he knew it was the best all around. So he pulled on his running shoes and headed down the stairs to the kitchen.

They were at his place this time because late last night Tori had wanted to try the Ketchums' hot air fryer. The remains of a really badly done chicken were littered over the counter. Another assortment of eclectic beer bottles were gathered in the recycling bin.

He smiled as he saw them, as pleased by the memories of Tori recounting her PhD difficulties as he was by the mind-blowing sex. He liked talking to her and that made for a happy summer.

He grabbed one of his green smoothies, downing it quickly while he started to stretch. Minutes later, he was out the door already thinking of the ways he was going to wake Tori when he came back all hot and sweaty.

He ran for an hour, but every step was about her. About what he intended to do to her later today. About what they could do together tonight. About what she might want to do...

His feet slowed as he headed back down the street to his house. There was Edward leaning on Tori's doorbell, a look of worry on his face.

Mike thought about turning around and going the other way, but just as he slowed to pivot, Edward started banging on the door. "Come on, Tori," Edward whined. "Wake up."

Jesus. How long had he been there? Couldn't be long. The man didn't have the patience to stand there without making more noise.

Mike was still trying to decide exactly what he was going to do when Edward spotted him. "Mike! I'm glad you're up! I can't get a hold of Tori."

Might as well deal with the guy now. He slowed to a walk and made it to the base of Tori's driveway. From this angle, he could see that the man had a bag of bagels and two coffees from the cheapo place down the street.

"Do you think she's hurt herself?" Edward asked, his voice tight with anxiety.

"I think she's asleep."

Edward rolled his eyes. "Of course she's sleeping. The woman likes her zzzzzs. But she isn't answering her phone and she's—"

"Maybe she's sleeping somewhere else."

Edward's face paled. He'd thought the man pasty-faced already, but one suggestion that Tori had someone else and the guy went whiter than a ghost. Mike had the urge to tell him to stick his head between his knees. Then Edward ruined all sense of sympathy by opening his mouth.

"You were supposed to call me if she found someone else."

"You were supposed to give her some space and not bang on her door at seven a.m. And I told you, I'm not keeping track of her dates."

"I have been giving her space! I am giving— Mike, tell me the truth. Is she seeing someone else?"

No way. Not a prayer he was going to give this dick more information. "You have got to let her look around some. Once she sees her options, maybe she'll see how wonderful you are." He almost choked on the words, but forced them through anyway. Anything to get this jerk out of Tori's life. "And maybe you can look around, too. Maybe there's someone other—"

"No!" Edward rubbed a distracted hand over his face. "I have been looking around, I've even gone on some dates but…I thought letting Tori come here would show her… That she'd learn… Oh hell…" The man was practically babbling in his misery.

Mike reluctantly took a few steps forward. "Calm down. You're going to wake the entire neighborhood."

Edward took a deep breath, then turned his tortured gaze to Mike. "I didn't realize how much I need her. I didn't think she was so essential to me. I…I… You have no idea what the last few weeks have been like." He lifted his hands in a defeated gesture. "I miss her every minute of every day. My work has suffered. I've gained seven pounds, and yesterday, I couldn't even play Civilization without crying."

Oh shit. The guy really was a basket case. That shouldn't make a difference to Mike, but it did. He felt an unwelcome twinge of sympathy because how awful would it be to have had years with Tori and screw it up? To realize too late just what you'd lost.

He wiped the sweat off his forehead. "Start with a phone call. Leave her a message. See if she'll…I don't know…go to lunch with you." After all, the man wasn't going to be having breakfast bagels with her.

Edward shook his head. "I tried that. I've been calling for days."

Really? "And?"

"She ignores them. She ignores me." That was obviously a shock to the guy.

Mike sighed. He really ought to put the man out of his misery. "Look, there's no easy way to say this, but she's met someone."

Edward leaned heavily against the cracked siding. "Who is it? Is he…you know…attractive?"

Mike barely restrained his grin. Might as well admit the truth. "Yeah. He's ripped."

"But is he smart? Tori would see through a dumb guy in a heartbeat."

Mike shrugged. "Don't know. Doesn't matter. She's with him now."

Edward straightened, his expression turning almost fierce. "It does matter because I'm not done. I'm going to marry her, you know. I just have to…" He gestured up toward the house. "I just have to get her to see me."

There it was. The face of true love, at least as it looked on Edward. The guy really had it bad for Tori, and Mike hadn't the heart to crush him. Worse, he knew just the right advice to give the guy. And though the words actually hurt going through his mouth, he said them anyway.

"The guy isn't hanging around. Five weeks and he's gone."

"He's a summer fling?"

Mike winced even though that was exactly what he was. "Yeah. Wait until the fall. Let her…" Was he really going to say this? "Let her get him out of her system. Then when he's gone—"

"I can console her. I can be the big man who then gives her what she's always wanted."

Mike looked up. "And what's that?"

"A ring. A house. You know, two-point-five kids and a white picket fence."

He frowned, thinking about that. Tori already had the house and she could install the white picket fence if she really wanted it. But the husband and kids… Well, that was something that required a man. Someone who shared her lifestyle and her goals. Like Edward, who was an academic like her. Not someone who was on the road half the year and whose only goal was to keep scoring baskets until they dragged his crippled body off the court.

In terms of staying power, clearly Edward was the better choice—though not by much. And it's not like Tori had the choice of just the two of them. There were lots of other academics in the world who weren't douchebags. Someone else could give her everything she deserved.

He looked back at his house and pictured his woman snoring into his pillow. "Just wait until fall," he said softly. "You'll only piss her off if you badger her now."

He looked back to where Edward was clearly thinking hard. "But maybe I should stick around? You know, give her the coffee and the bagels? Maybe I'll find something out about this guy."

"Trust me," Mike said, "you don't want to know. Physically, he's a god."

"Really? In Evanston?"

"People work out, Edward. Even people who live in the burbs." He looked at the guy's thin legs. "You should try it sometime. You're going to have to compete against this guy in bed."

Edward waved his hand in dismissal. "All those steroid dicks are flabby in bed. I assure you, I can compete."

Having never taken a steroid in his life, he couldn't speak to that. Though he certainly knew that Edward hadn't been remotely adequate in bed. In fact, Mike had just decided to spend the rest of his summer making sure no one ever came close to his prowess in that area. And certainly not this lightweight.

Meanwhile, he gestured to the food. "You should go. I'll make sure she gets these."

Edward hesitated, clearly undecided. So Mike pushed him over the edge.

"You don't want to stand next to this man. Physically, man, you just don't measure up."

Edward stiffened. "There're other assets beyond a physique. Things that I have in abundance. I have a good job that pays me well."

So did Mike. Millions every year. But eventually his playing years would be over, whereas Edward probably had tenure. He'd be employed for decades, well after Mike was a crippled old geezer. And as if Edward could read his mind, he kept talking, rubbing salt into the wound.

"Tori and I understand each other's fields. We can talk about our professional lives."

Crap. Tori had certainly been studying basketball, but what the hell did he know about comparative religion? In this particular case, Edward had it over him in spades.

"Plus she likes my friends. And they like her."

Mike winced, thinking of what she would think of his friends. That they were all big dumb jocks, probably. And crude as well. And though his sisters were well on their way to higher degrees, their background was vastly different from Tori's ivory tower life. Hell, he didn't even know his real father. Hers came over for sushi and pie.

"Tori needs to be with me," Edward said firmly. Clearly the man had just convinced himself it was true.

"So wait until she gets tired of the mundane assets and impress her with your other attributes."

The man still wasn't convinced, but Mike was now beyond tired of this conversation. He didn't make a habit of measuring himself against other men, but Edward was making him do it with an unusually clear eye. Except for the really hot sex, what did he and Tori have in common?

Nothing.

"Look, I'm going to take a shower. You want me to give her those bagels or not?"

Edward gave in with little grace. He shoved the bagels at him and one of the coffees. "It's all her favorites in there. Even the strawberry cream cheese. This is her favorite mocha. It had whip cream and sprinkles too, but it's probably all melted."

Mike grabbed the bag and coffee, doing his best not to throw them at the guy. Jesus, he didn't want Tori to want this bastard, but he had to let her make the choice. He had to let her live her life even if it meant she chose a dickhead instead of… Of what? Him? Life on the road, hanging out with basketball jocks and their bunny wives? She'd hate all the publicity and the lack of privacy. Sure, she'd handled the one guy in the restaurant with poise. But how would she deal with dozens of them banging on their door every day? He'd seen strong women crack under that kind of pressure.

"I'll tell her," Mike said as he turned for his house. And Tori.

"Tell her I'll call her. That, you know, I'd like to take her out to lunch or something."

Not even a candlelight dinner. How cheap could one man be?

"Tell her I'm saving up my money to buy her a really big ring."

Ouch. It was a good thing Mike was at his front door because he really wanted to deck the guy. Instead, he gave the bastard a half-hearted wave and pushed into the house. And just to put the icing on the crapola cake, Tori was there at the living room window. She'd been watching the whole exchange. But how much had she heard?

He looked at her blank face wishing he could read her mind. He couldn't, so he held up the bag and cup. "Offerings from Edward."

"Yeah, I saw."

Then she closed her eyes. "Let me guess. A mocha with whip cream and sprinkles."

He nodded.

"Moron."

"What?"

"And the bagels are blueberry, French toast, and cinnamon apple crunch. With strawberry cream cheese."

They were moving together to the kitchen, so he couldn't look. But the cream cheese was right. "Aren't those your favorites?"

She shook her head. "They're his favorites. But to be fair, I don't think I've ever really told him my preference. I'm just not all that excited about bagels."

"What about the mocha?"

She shook her head. "Too sweet. I like almond milk lattes." She shrugged. "He probably called his mother for advice. She's the one who loves mochas."

Mike set down the bag and looked inside. Yup, she'd called the bagels spot on. "He called his mother for dating advice?"

"It's not like his friends have a clue." When he looked up at her, she shrugged. "Geeks and posers, most of them. Though there are a few who are really sweet."

"So you don't like his friends?"

She reached forward and pulled out a bagel, grimaced, then tossed it back. "They're fine." Then when he was silent for a beat, she looked back at him. "I don't really like a lot of people, Mike. Just about everyone is fine. Some more annoying, others less."

"Fine."

She nodded, then she stepped closer to him. "Others are really *fine*." She drew out the word, making it sound luxurious. Like a fine wine or fine dark chocolate. On her lips, the word was sexy, and he couldn't help the response of his body. His dick thickened and his hand wrapped around her waist, drawing her close before he remembered that he was hot and sweaty. And not in a fine way.

"Damn. Let me take a shower."

"Don't you remember? You're really hot when you're sweaty."

"And…" He cut off his words. There were too many other things competing for his attention. Like the way her hair looked like summer wheat in the sunshine where it wasn't touched with gold. Like the way she always smelled like lemons and spice to him. Like… "Take one with me," he said.

She grinned. "Okay. Then I'll make you an omelet for breakfast."

He nuzzled the side of her neck, nipping the skin just enough to make her shiver. "Take a shower with me and then we'll go out for breakfast. I'll have a French chef make you the best omelet of your life."

"I can cook one, you know. And not burn the eggs."

He straightened. "I know. But why would you when I can

buy—"

"Are you avoiding my cooking or trying to treat me?"

"Can't it be both?" It was a joke. Even Tori couldn't screw up a basic omelet. Then he sobered. "Honestly, I just want to give you the best while—" He slammed his mouth shut, narrowly missing his own tongue.

She sobered. "While we're together," she finished for him.

God, he hated the ticking bomb hanging over their relationship. They were together for the rest of the summer, and then… Then she would be free to go back to Edward or whatever damned pasty-faced prick she wanted.

She touched his lips with her fingers then extended the caress up his face. She stroked his cheekbone and over the curve of his ear. "In ten years, Mike, what's your plan then?"

"To look back on a glorious career." It was a knee-jerk response. That was his pat answer whenever he thought about the end of his basketball days. It was the only way he could deal with the clutching panic that came with the idea of the end of professional basketball. But Tori was smarter than the average reporter and she wasn't about to let him get off with an automatic response.

"You don't have to tell me if you don't want to. I just wondered."

But he did want to tell her. When he usually ran screaming from the very thought, he suddenly wanted to talk out the details with her. To get her opinion. To wonder if maybe he was just blowing smoke up his own ass. After all, he'd already built to the top of one career. Only sheer arrogance made him think he could do it again in another field. One that didn't involve a big body or amazing ball skills.

"That's not a small question, Tori. It's going to take me a while to answer it."

"We've got all summer."

He chuckled, catching her hand so he could press a kiss

into her fingers. "How about I tell you over omelets?"

"Hmmm," she said, while he nipped at the tips of her fingers. "After the shower, right?"

"Yeah. After the shower." And whatever other fun and games they happened to do.

"Okay." She stretched up on her toes to nip at his lips. Not a kiss, but a tiny bite that might have been painful if she'd misjudged the distance. But she had it right, just as she had a way with giving him an incentive to do something uncomfortable. "I'll make you a deal. I'll make your shower especially memorable if you tell me about your plan at breakfast."

He caught her chin. "Every shower with you is memorable."

"I said *especially* mem—"

"Deal."

She grinned. "Just give me a second to get it ready." Then she dashed upstairs. He had no idea what she meant to do, but damned if he wasn't hot and hard just thinking of possibilities.

One summer, he told himself. If he only had the summer with her, then he was going to make damn sure he lived every second to the fullest.

Even if it meant he spilled his guts while eating overpriced eggs.

Chapter Fifteen

Tori knew that good sex worked up an appetite. Apparently, phenomenal sex made her ravenous. Fortunately, the very best pancake house in the country was not so far from her. Great omelets. Great fresh squeezed orange juice. And best of all, they were past the morning rush and not on a weekend. That meant a quiet booth in the back where she could pick Mike's brain to her heart's content.

Unfortunately, he seemed more interested in filling his gut than spilling it. So she put down her fork, drained her coffee, then fixed him with her most intimidating teacher stare.

It took him a moment to notice, but when he did, he started laughing. "You really are cute when you try to looking threatening."

"It's a devastating combination: cute menace. Is it working?"

He set down his fork. "Maybe."

"Good. So spill."

"Tori, I'm really not that deep. I don't have any dark secrets—"

"But you do have plans. Like I have stray thoughts, you have plans. So what's your five-year plan?"

"Basketball. Two more championship rings."

She frowned a bit. "Why not five?"

He snorted as he grabbed his juice. "Plans are supposed to be a stretch, not pie-in-the-sky impossible."

She shook her head. Whenever she made plans, she always shot for the stars. Saved her the effort of actually being realistic. Which is another reason she never went for long-term thinking.

"So glorious basketball for another ten years."

He nodded.

"Then what?"

He was silent, staring at the remains of his omelet. She let him think for a bit. She knew he had plans, but obviously he needed to work up the courage to tell her.

"I swear I won't tell," she said.

He looked up, startled. "That's not it. I've never put this into words before. I don't like thinking about it even in my own head."

"That scary?"

"I was never good at school. Not bad, but not..." He gestured at her with his finger. "Not your kind of smart."

She snorted. "My kind of smart is simply being anti-social. I like to learn and I don't like hanging around with a lot of people."

"You do just fine with me."

"You're a lot of guy, not a lot of people."

He grinned, then took a deep breath. When he spoke, the words came out all in a rush. "I want to go back to school, Tori. I want to learn how to manage money for a charitable trust."

Well that wasn't what she expected. She'd been guessing endorsement deals, coaching, or something to do with basketball. "You're talking an MBA. In finance, I think. But you don't need a degree to run a charity."

"I know. But it helps."

She dropped her chin on her hand. "What kind of charity?"

"Boys and Girls Club. I've visited different facilities, talked to the kids. I didn't have one when I was growing up. Obviously it hasn't hurt me, but it could have helped my friends. Girls who got pregnant because they were bored, guys who started drinking or doing drugs for the same reason. Kids need a place to go when school's out. I thought I could help with that."

"You don't have to wait ten years to do that."

"I already donate, but I want to get involved. I want to really reach those kids who need some guidance and a lot of structure."

She leaned back, trying to understand why it was so secretive. "That's great, Mike."

He flashed her a wan smile. She waited, but he didn't say more. Eventually she had to ask.

"I don't understand. Why are you acting so weird about it?"

"Tori...I don't just want to run the charity. I want to work every day in it. And I want to support it with my money, too."

She nodded. "I got that."

"Most of my money. You think that because I make millions in a year, I'm going to be rolling in it all my life. I'll never be poor, but I keep myself to a strict budget. I've never wanted a flashy lifestyle, so the rest goes to—"

"Your charity. I get it."

"I wish. I've got family to support. My sisters are getting their graduate degrees. My mother has lots of medical expenses."

"I'm sorry—"

"And my cousins are always around looking for a handout. I've got a business manager, and one of the things he does is track the freeloader part of my family. I pay them to work at a Boys and Girls Club. If they want my help, then they have to work for it."

She kept her mouth shut, waiting for him to explain. But he stopped talking and after he'd drained his orange juice he just sat there with a sullen expression.

"I'm still waiting for why this is so bad. Why are you angry?"

"I'm not angry," he said, his tone curt. She arched her brows, and eventually he sighed. "People only see the game part of my job. They don't see the practice, the daily nutrition, the work of all that media bullshit. Do you know they want me to have a website updated weekly, and social media that gets an hourly message?"

She tried to think back. "I've never seen you tweet. And your Facebook page hasn't been touched since last season. Well, not by you." His fans posted all the time.

"I know. I hate that stuff. I didn't used to, but it gets to be a grind. I've hired someone to help with it and he's working with the media people about my come-back this fall."

"How much do you have to do for that?"

He huffed out a breath. "As little as possible. But they like the story. Injured in a charity tournament, has it cost him his career? Buy tickets now and see the end live and in person!"

"That's not what they're saying."

"Of course it is. Everyone wants to know if basketball is over for me." He leaned forward. "Tori, no one cares if I just play well. I have to be spectacular somehow. Either with phenomenal play or a glorious disaster."

She dropped her chin into her hand as she dredged up what little she knew about sports and the culture around it. "I don't think that's true. The fans just want to watch you play."

"I don't work for the fans," he said softly. "I work for the guys who want me to sell tickets."

Ah. There it was. Sure everyone wanted him to win games, but money was harder and harder to come by. The owners of the team paid Mike very well to sell tickets. That meant putting on a show. Add that to the pressure of being at the top of his physical ability despite his age and injuries, and that added up to a whole lot of pressure.

"You're handling it very well."

"I—" He shrugged. "I like the pressure. It keeps me sharp."

"Doesn't it get exhausting?"

"That's why I'm hiding out in Evanston this summer."

"But in the fall you're going back to it."

He flashed a quick smile. "Yeah."

So he loved it, too. He had to, she supposed, otherwise he wouldn't be so good at it. "And every time I ask you about your ten-year plan, you think about what will end your basketball career. What will happen that makes it impossible to play anymore?" She leaned forward. "So your anxiety has nothing to do with whether or not you can run a charity."

"Yeah, it does. Damn it, Tori, I was a nutrition major in college. And not a very good one."

She blinked. She had no idea that had been his field of study. Everything she'd read had been about his amazing basketball ability. "Now there's a field that needs people."

He snorted. "Not why I studied it. It was all about peak performance—mine. And that in no way prepared me to run a charity."

She waved that away with her fork. "Compared to what you've been doing—are still doing—that's nothing. Hell, if you can learn whether to balance fish protein with vegetable fats, then—"

"Okay, so that's clearly not your field of study."

"—managing a charitable trust will be a breeze." She sobered as she looked at him. "You know I don't care about your money one way or the other."

He frowned at his plate and then nodded slowly. "It's a rare woman who doesn't like the idea of hanging out with a rich guy."

"I make my own money, thank you very much, Mr. Millionaire. But you're right, I'm a rare woman," she said with a grin.

He looked up at her. "It's one of the reasons I like you, but…" He snapped his mouth shut, clearly regretting what he was about to say.

"But what?"

"But this is my vacation. How are you going to handle the media circus that is my life later?"

That was a question, all right. One that she had no idea how to answer. Except that… "The circus is in New York."

He nodded. "And you're here."

"So are you…for now."

"For now," he echoed.

That was it. The certain understanding that their lives were very different. And at the end of the summer, they would go their separate ways.

"When it's time," she said, "when you want to go back to school, give me a call. I know some people who might be able to help you."

"That's a long way off, Tori."

"I know. At least a decade, right?" Unless he got injured.

"At least."

She looked away, hating herself for wishing he had a career-ending injury just so they could stay in this summer forever. So to counteract her negative thoughts, she voiced her wish out loud. "I hope you shock everyone and play well into your fifties."

He barked out a laugh. "Pie-in-the-sky planning."

"My favorite kind."

He grinned and she felt a little better. He was smiling now which meant it was time to head back to their perfect summer.

"So what should we do today? I'm thinking of designing a labyrinth for my backyard."

"What, no Minotaur?"

"Of course I'd have a Minotaur. He'd be a really ugly statue in the middle."

"Wouldn't the treasure be in the middle? He's the defense so he should be lurking around the corner somewhere."

She pursed her lips. "I suppose you're right. Come on, let's go search for garden statues."

He chuckled as he gathered up the bill. "So long as it's not a gnome, I'm game."

"Then we have a problem, Mike," she said in mock seriousness. "Because the scariest Minotaurs are ugly gnomes."

He was still laughing as they made it to the car. She kept him chuckling all through the garden store and the rock store and the high-end liquor store—she was running low on specialty beer. But every time she got him to laugh, part of her wondered what it would be like to never hear that again. To look back in just two months and realize that they would never be like this again.

Answer: It sucked. Big time.

She was still mulling that depressing thought over when they made it to home.

"Who's that?" Mike asked. It was the tone of his voice that pulled her out of her reverie. A little tight and a lot wary.

"Where?"

Mike gestured and she saw a lanky man stretched out on her front porch with his arm over his eyes. He was wearing ripped cutoffs that exposed his knobby knees and big feet where one of his flip-flops had fallen off. And he looked like he was sleeping.

"Don't worry. He's got a Northwestern tee on. See the purple?"

"Because undergrads can't be crazy," Mike muttered as he pushed open the car door.

She followed, grabbing a bag of groceries before she started for her front door. Mike grabbed the other three. "He's not a Northwestern student. Just wears it to be nice to me."

"Only thing that's clean 'cause I'm too ashamed to wear it," the man muttered without moving his arm.

"So that smell is you?" she asked as she stepped over him.

"Har, har."

"Mike, meet my brother Duncan. He's come to check up on me." Even though he was her favorite sibling, she couldn't keep the irritation out of her tone.

Meanwhile, her brother lifted his arm off his face then scowled at Mike. "Am I still drunk?"

"Are you breathing?" she quipped.

"Har har," he repeated as he pulled together his sprawled limbs and struggled to sit up.

Tori ignored him and pushed through her front door. Mike on the other hand remained right where he was, scowling down at her brother.

"Are you usually drunk on a Saturday afternoon?" he challenged.

"It's my first thought when looking face to face with a celebrity NY Knick. Jesus, does Jess know that you're the friendly neighbor? And if not, can I please be the one to tell her?"

Tori didn't answer. She didn't care what her sister knew or who told her. Instead she busied herself putting away the beer, then her eyes caught on her backyard and she lost herself to thoughts of the labyrinth she might create back there. It was all a way to distract herself from the end of the summer which was still a long way away. And yet, standing there, she couldn't seem to think of anything else.

"Earth to Tori," came her brother's voice.

"I'm alive. Now go away," she returned, her voice harder than it would normally be, but her thoughts had turned sour and it came out in her words.

Then Mike was beside her, his hand large and warm as he trailed it down her arm. "You know," he said, "you'd think a woman's family would respect her accomplishments."

"It's okay, Mike," Tori murmured. She was well used to her family's condescension where she was concerned.

"It's not okay. Family coming to say, 'Hey, how ya doing?' is one thing. Drunk on your front step and talking crap is another."

He was defending her. She didn't need it, but she couldn't deny the warm joy that washed through her that he would stand up to her family for her. Unfortunately, it was wasted on the wrong family member.

"Duncan's not drunk."

"Yeah," her brother said as he swiped a beer from her fridge. "At least not yet."

Mike grabbed it out of his hand and set it on the counter. "A guest asks."

Tori smiled. He was becoming a regular papa bear on her behalf and she thought it wonderful. Meanwhile, Duncan smiled too sweetly at her.

"Mother, may I?"

"You driving?"

"Yes."

"Then no."

He scowled at her but she decided to gesture at the now finished living room floor. "I'm not dead, the house is coming along, and you can report back to everyone that I'm doing fine."

"I'm going to tell everyone about your neighbor." He plopped down on her kitchen stool and grabbed a yogurt, asking for permission with a raised eyebrow. She nodded, and as he popped open the lid, he scanned the flooring behind her. "Nice job. And I'm only here because Jess promised to help with my tuition if I did."

Tori spun around, startled out of her relationship thoughts. "You need money for tuition? What happened?"

Her brother grinned at her. "Nothing. Doesn't mean I won't take money from Jess."

It took a moment for her to understand what was going on. Her brother had his own unique sense of humor, but when she did, she started chuckling. And a moment later, she took the time to explain it to Mike.

"Duncan just finished his second tour in the Navy. He's now in law school at the University of Chicago, and contrary to what everyone in the family seems to think, he squirrels away his money like it's gold."

"My needs are simple."

"He's cheap," Tori corrected. "But it works for him. The more he looks like he's on his last dime, the more the relatives throw money at him."

"Same with your helpless act," Duncan shot back. Then he turned to Mike. "All her life, she's pretended to be clueless so people would stop trying to bring her into their drama. It works. No one ever bothers her."

"You're bothering me."

He shrugged. "'Cause I wanted to know why you suddenly need to stand on your own." He knocked the yogurt cup back, draining it like a thick smoothie. Then when he was done, he dropped it onto the counter and looked hard at her. "What's going on, sis?"

She sighed, not knowing how to answer in words. The

thoughts were too vague in her own mind to answer her brother. Especially since he was the one who could most see through her bullshit.

But then her eyes connected with Mike's. He had stayed by her side, silently witnessing the byplay between her and Duncan, but at her pleading look, he tucked her tighter to his side. "Sometimes you just gotta throw out everything and start over," he said.

Mike understood. She hadn't thought he'd had enough time with her to see the truth, but apparently, she'd been wrong. He understood her all too well.

Duncan appeared to think about that. "Scorched Earth maneuver, huh? Problem is, you can't ever go back. You prove to everyone that you're extremely capable and they'll expect you to remember lunch dates and the like." He let his voice trail off suggestively, but she just shook her head. She hadn't a clue what he was trying to say.

Fortunately, Mike was there to translate. "Did you forget a lunch date, maybe? Other than the one with your father?"

"No," she murmured, thinking about her schedule. "That's not until… Oh shit. Duncan I'm sorry."

"And there's the Tori we all know."

"Why didn't you email me?"

Her brother didn't answer. Just arched a brow at her.

Right. She hadn't checked her email. Not for a few days. "I've been busy," she said, gesturing again at the floor even though she knew it was a lame excuse.

"I can see that," her brother answered, his gaze on Mike.

Well, yes, that too. Meanwhile, her brother straightened off the kitchen stool, adjusted his flip-flops with a casual flick of his toes, and then tossed the empty yogurt carton into the trash. "I know how you can make it up to me."

"Yeah? How?"

"I've got a bet with Jess. I told her you'd have this house

renovated by the end of the summer. That it'd be perfectly habitable and you'd do it without a single emergency trip visit."

She blinked, startled. "Even I won't bet on that." Not given the fall off the roof, the disaster with the electrical system, and that didn't begin to count what she intended to do with the kitchen.

"I would," Mike said, his voice calm. "What're the terms?"

Duncan's face broke out into a wide grin. "That's the best part. She loses, she goes out on a blind date with one of my friends."

Tori didn't stop her snort of laughter. "Isn't that kind of cruel?"

"Hey!" he protested. "I've got lots of nice friends."

Mike slanted a look at her. "I think she meant cruel to your friend." God, it was great when someone got her sense of humor.

"Oh right." Duncan waggled his eyebrows. "Well that's fair, I suppose. I've got some friends I'd like to torture, too."

Tori laughed, but her gaze was looking about her house. There were so many things she'd like to do. "If I focus on the house, I'd never get the labyrinth done in time."

Her brother made a choking sound. "Labyrinth? In your postage stamp of a backyard?"

"But on the other hand," offered Mike, "you could pull down the chicken wallpaper and paint while it's still breezy enough to open up your house to air it out."

"Very true," she said, though in her mind she substituted other words. It wasn't that it would be warm enough to air out the paint smells. It's that she would have another place to sleep—with him—while it dried. "But I've grown fond of the chickens."

"It does make a statement," Mike agreed.

"But it clashes with the Bast motifs."

Mike grinned. "Chickens and cats never do well together."

She sighed. "All right, Duncan. Go ahead and find an enemy you wish to torture on a blind date with Jess."

"Ooh," he said, rubbing his hands together, "the possibilities are endless." Then he flashed her a smile. "I'll tell them to come here for a barbecue in a month. That should be plenty of time, right?"

"A month?" she cried. She couldn't possibly have her new furniture by then. She hadn't decided if she wanted to go lounge comfortable to make the place inviting or stay away minimalist to deliver a clear message to her relations.

"It'll be great. Can't wait," her brother said as he pushed through the front door. The screen door banged behind him.

Meanwhile, she looked at Mike, doubt crowding her mind. "There's a lot to do in a month."

"I'll help, if you want."

"Of course I want. It's lots more fun with you." Assuming they didn't get distracted into more fun activities.

"Good, because I think you should plan on cooking for the party."

She frowned. "Whatever for?"

He grinned. "What about sushi?"

Oh! "Great idea." She loved it that he understood her so well.

Especially since a month of house renovations, sushi practice, and great sex would keep her mind off how quickly the summer would fly by.

Chapter Sixteen

The end came sooner than either of them expected. A month of hot sex, weird beer, and home repair had put Mike in such a good frame of mind that he hadn't stressed about his shoulder. And that meant he didn't overtrain it during recovery, which meant it healed fast.

Really fast. Which made him even happier.

Until his fourth barbecue of the summer and the grand unveiling of Tori's renovated house. The place was an eclectic masterpiece of everything that was her, and her family had been suitably impressed. The kitchen chickens were gone, replaced by sleek white appliances, a butter yellow wall, and an elegant Bast goddess watercolor she'd found on the internet. The furniture was comfortable, the fabrics unexpectedly soft given their nubby texture, but it was all done in a cushioned rattan that was both relaxing and a little uninviting given that it was so bizarre to find in northern Illinois. Tori had said that was exactly the look she was going for, so he could only applaud her decision.

And the piece de resistance? Together, they had indeed created her labyrinth, but out of decorative stones laid out in an elaborate multi-color array. Right now her brother and sister were walking the path while Duncan described a variety of disastrous date possibilities to Jessica. Last he'd checked, the poor woman had gone green beneath her elegantly casual makeup.

Meanwhile, Tori was serving fabulous sushi while his friends clustered around the display of specialty beers that he and Tori had selected from their summer of exploration. He'd worried at first that Tori would be bored—or worse, disdainful—of his Chicago-based friends. Not so much. At the very first barbeque, Joey had tried his best pick-up lines on Tori and she'd shot him down by suggesting he'd have better luck with dumber women. That had made her a favorite with his set. Plus, she'd decided to do a study of the mythology behind lucky rituals in sports, and the women of the group were all about telling details that set everyone laughing.

Until tonight. It was hot as hell in Illinois. No tempering breezes off Lake Michigan, just humidity. So they were mostly gathered around her living room, drinking exotic beer while Tori's father laughed at sports jokes that he might or might not understand. The women were in the kitchen area talking aboriginal cooking rituals. That was Tori. The others were holding their sides they were laughing so hard as she tried to act one out.

Then Tori brought out more homemade sushi. Most of it had already been served, but she'd discovered the tray that had gone missing because it was in a covered tray behind the lemonade and buried by a couple bags of chips.

"Darling," her mother said as she came down the stairs from inspecting the upper floor. "We shouldn't eat that. It's supposed to be served as soon as it's made." She spoke in crisp accents that perfectly complemented her pristine linen suit and tightly coifed hair. By contrast, Tori wore cutoffs and a graphic tee that said, *Atheism: a non prophet organization.* Her hair hung in Mike's favorite loose and a bit wild style.

"It is just made," Tori answered. "About an hour ago."

"But dear, it's sushi. You wouldn't want to make your guests sick."

Mike moved nearby, but knew better than to interfere. Tori could handle herself and she wouldn't appreciate him coming to the rescue.

"Thanks for the input Mom, and you're right. If you're worried, you shouldn't have any." She shifted the tray over to the opposite side of the table where Cole was sitting. Cole was the Knicks' star center and he was as big as a house. He was also visiting his sister in Chicago, so had dropped in. His expression lifted when Tori set the tray right beside him.

"Are these all for me?"

"Nope. For your expert opinion."

His lips curved which startled Mike. The man was typically silent off the court and lately had tended to morose. Something dark was up with the man, but suddenly the guy was nearing a smile as he looked at Tori. Mike made a point of moving a step closer to her and setting his hand on her shoulder. It wasn't needed. Cole would never poach, but damn it, the man attracted women like flies to honey. It was something about the mystery of a quiet giant.

Meanwhile, Cole lifted up the tray to inspect every sushi offering with a critical eye. He inhaled delicately then started asking questions that were over everyone else's head. About where she'd gotten the fish, the knife she'd used, even the nature and quality of the rice. Tori answered them all with a calm, clear voice.

And then the moment of truth. Cole grabbed a pair of chopsticks, picked up a piece of the most complicated roll on the tray, and made a show of eating it. He didn't even use soy or wasabi, but ate it dry. The man might be quiet, but he still knew how to put on a show.

His eyes closed as he chewed slowly.

Swallow.

Silence.

Then he opened his eyes and looked to the tray. Picking up the most simple offering of nigiri he repeated the process while everyone waited, breath held.

Then he held out his hand, and Tori was right there putting a cup of tea into his massive palm. "The tea is crap," Tori said, "but it's all I have."

Cole took a sip and grimaced. "Ugh. That's awful."

"I know. I'm sorry—"

"You should not serve this swill," he pushed aside the tea, "with such perfect sushi. What were you thinking?"

Tori laughed. "That I didn't know you were coming so didn't have time to go to Chinatown." Then she took a step forward. "So I pass?"

"Darling," he drawled, mimicking her mother's posh tone. "I would let you serve this at Hai Sun's."

Everyone in the kitchen rushed forward to grab a piece. Everyone, of course, but her mother who had curled her lip in disdain. "Just because a man eats a lot of sushi—"

"Mom, have I introduced you to Cole West, star center for the NY Knicks?"

"Hello Mr. West—"

"In addition to his amazing athletic ability, he's also a sushi chef, graduate of the Tokyo Sushi Academy, and part owner of Hai Sung, the most elite Japanese restaurant in Los Angeles. He worked there all through high school and bought in later." Then she patted her mother's hand. "But you're right. I wouldn't just trust anyone's sushi, especially if it's been sitting out."

"But," added Cole, "a good chef knows the limits of her cooking and her ingredients. And you are an exquisite chef." He held out a hand to Tori who flushed prettily as she set her hand into his. Then he kissed the back of it like a suitor from the 1800s.

"Okay, okay," Mike said, drawing Tori to his side. "We all know you're special. No need to go showing it off." Of all the men on the team, Cole was the best educated. Like everyone else, he'd entered the draft before finishing college, but he'd taken exams to finish out the classes he needed. He'd studied at home and flew back to school to take the exams. Add to that his chef and restaurant credentials, and he had a full restaurateur career available to him if he ever decided to give up basketball.

And then something happened. Something that shocked everyone enough to stare.

Cole grinned. Not a curve of his lips, but a full-out, white teeth bared grin. Sure, everyone here had seen that hundreds of times, but only on the court. Only there did the guy ever let his emotions fully out.

Except right here, right now.

It was so startling that Doc paused with a piece of nigiri halfway to his mouth. "Dude, are you feeling all right?"

Cole turned, and that was it. The spell was broken and his neutral face returned. "I'm fine, why?"

Doc scrambled for an answer. What could he say? We're all so shocked you smiled? That would be rude. So he shrugged and mumbled, "Nothing. Just liked seeing those pearly whites, is all."

It might have been awkward, but Tori was there with a glass of her lemonade. "This isn't tea," she said softly, "but it is fresh."

Cole accepted it with a gracious nod, but that was the last anyone saw of his pearly whites. It might have put a gloom over the party. It certainly quieted that little corner of the room for a moment. But then Joey showed up and put the axe on the entire event.

After being shot down by Tori a month ago, Joey'd starting bringing dates. A different bimbo each time. Except for tonight when he showed up alone with a drawn expression and an apologetic look. Mike felt every cell in his body tighten even as he turned to greet the guy. He meant to say, "Hey there, you're late." Or maybe, "Couldn't find a girl drunk enough to join you tonight?" Something light enough to keep with the celebratory mood. Instead, he said the five words that had plagued him all summer.

"What's wrong with my shoulder?"

Joey drew up short one step into the living room. "What? Nothing!" His expression turned sheepish. "You just haven't been answering your phone."

Very true. He had wanted to wring every moment out of his time with Tori, so he'd taken to leaving his phone at his house. He hadn't looked at it in two days.

"Um, so who's been calling?"

"Your boss."

Oh shit.

"Coach or…"

Joey shook his head. That meant it was Mr. James Dolan, the owner. His gaze went to Tori's and she smiled sweetly at him. Everything she did was sweet, but in this case it was especially clueless. She didn't know what a call from the team's owner meant.

"So I guess I should, uh, go check my messages."

"No need. The message is to call him right back."

Right. "So why'd he call you?"

Joey glanced at Tori, then he sighed. "I had to tell him your shoulder was okay. Not quite good as new, but good enough to play."

"Well of course you had to tell him that." He hadn't actually been hiding his shoulder recovery. He just hadn't been anxious to get back to the East Coast.

Joey held out his phone. "Call him on mine. That way he knows I got you the message."

Right. And it made sure that Mike called back right then

and there. "You think I could wait until tomorrow?"

"Absolutely not."

Well, that's what came of being paid millions of dollars a year. The man who signed the checks expected you to jump when he called. He looked at the phone. Joey had even keyed in the phone number for him. Great. He pressed dial and lifted the phone to his ear.

Mr. Dolan answered on the third ring.

"Hello, sir. It's Mike. I'm sorry. I've had, um, problems with my phone. What can I help you—"

Mr. Dolan didn't even let him finish his sentence. It was all about the new season, the publicity planned, and the fact that one of his teammates sprained an ankle. Which meant that the usual media frenzy was going to focus on him. It was everything he feared would happen. A big story about his surprise injury in his waning years.

Waning years. Jesus. It sounded like he was about to turn eighty.

"Sir, I'll be there in two weeks, just like we—"

Again, more words. Lots more words, but they all boiled down to "tomorrow." A flight at eight a.m. tomorrow from O'Hare. Which meant...

He looked to Tori. She flashed him another smile and for a moment he thought she didn't understand. But then she picked up the Nerf basketball they'd been playing with. She tossed it to him.

"Guess my rebound's over, huh?"

He nodded grimly. His boss was still talking. He listened with half an ear. All the rest of his body was completely and totally focused on Tori. And when the phone call was done, he passed the cell back to Joey before heading straight for Tori. "You'll come to my first game, right? I'll buy you season tickets. You can—"

"Of course I'll come. But you don't have—"

"For you and your dad."

She snorted and from the other room, her father called out, "I'm a Bulls fan."

Mike flashed him a wan smile. "Maybe I can convert you."

The man gave him a look that spelled *no way*. Meanwhile, Tori took hold of his hand. "What time do you have to leave?"

"Tomorrow. Early."

"Well then," said one of the women behind him. He didn't even care who. "I think we're going to call it a night. Right everybody?"

God bless his friends. He glanced over his shoulder, pleased when they all started gathering their things. But then he looked back to Tori and her name came out as a tortured groan.

She looked at him, her eyes steady and her shoulders excruciatingly stiff. A month ago he would have thought it a wide-eyed innocent look, but he'd been making a thorough study of his woman. She was gripping her hands together to keep them steady. And her jaw was clenched against her saying the wrong thing.

"So, um," he said softly. "I was hoping you could help me pack."

"Oh," she said, her voice small. "Is that what you really want?"

"It is. If you want to."

"Then…" She took a deep breath. "Then of course I'll help."

She did.

She helped him pack and promised to keep an eye on things until the Ketchums came back. And then they made love.

She cried when she came, turning her face away from him so he wouldn't see her tears.

But in the morning she was dry-eyed.

And he was the one who left.

Chapter Seventeen

They talked every night, but Mike could tell she was drifting away from him. That was the point, he supposed. After all, they'd both agreed to just be friends when the summer was over. But he'd thought they'd be *intimate* friends.

They'd tried, of course. When they spoke, she was right there with him, telling him about her day and asking about his. But even with Skype, they were missing something. The affectionate touches, the random thoughts that happened out of the blue, usually when she was just waking up. Between her preparations for the semester and his training schedule, they only had about an hour a day to be with each other over cyberspace. That left twenty-three other hours when she was doing stuff, seeing people, being Tori and he wasn't around.

It was killing him.

Almost as much as the training. He hadn't worked this hard since he'd been a freshman in high school trying to bulk up.

Everything in him was aimed at his first game. She was going to fly out for three days. She'd gotten someone to cover her classes and he was going to show her New York the way only a mega-rich superstar could. Her father was coming, too, and he'd already planned to give the old guy the full Knicks press. He was going to convert the man to a Knicks fan, and then he was going to let the man loose with the team while he spirited Tori away.

That was the plan, and he was giddy the day he finally waited in baggage claim, a dozen red roses in his arms and a Knicks jersey for her dad. His plan was simple: show her so good a time that she was open to relocating to out here. Maybe NYU needed a visiting professor or something. At least she could think about taking her sabbatical with him. Something. Anything. But it started with saying the words he'd held back for too long: I love you. I love you, please help me find a way for us to be together.

Hell, he'd even play for the Bulls if they'd take him.

Jesus, where was she? He was well known here, and as much as he'd tried to keep it quiet, there were already reporters "hanging out" in baggage claim. Some weren't even trying to be subtle, and he'd already given "no comment" to the few who asked who was getting the roses.

Damn it, he was getting nervous. This was like dropping Tori into the middle of a firestorm. The second he handed her the roses, she'd be swept up in the media whirlwind.

Come on. Come on. It was bad enough the flight had been delayed out of Chicago. He'd been waiting hours. Where—

He saw her. Blonde, slender, and beautiful. She seemed to light up the world. He was so happy to see her that he didn't at first register that she wasn't smiling. And she wasn't with her father.

Holy shit, what the hell was Edward doing here? And with his hand lying possessively on her lower back?

She saw him as soon as they topped the escalator. At least her reaction was just what he'd been imagining. Her face lit up with a huge grin and she started to push her way down the escalator, but there was no hope. It was too stuffed with people for her to go anywhere. So he got to just look at her— so animated she was bouncing—and his heart just swelled. Until Edward grinned and waved too.

Fuck. Fuck. Fuck.

Were they back together? They couldn't be. She hadn't said anything. Well, that wasn't exactly true. She said they'd had lunch a few times and gotten together for coffee. A movie one night, too. And that it was nice that he finally appreciated her.

God, no. It couldn't be possible, but the bastard was here and not her father.

She finally made it to the end of the escalator and ran full tilt at him. He tried to present her the roses, but didn't get the chance. She jumped into his arms—well, his free arm—and he held her so close that he lifted her off the ground.

He wanted to tell her to be careful. That there was press everywhere, but the words got lost. His mind was a haze of *ToriToriToriTori*. The way she smelled, the feel of her against his body, the way she breathed. Everything about her was right. Especially when she planted her mouth on his and kissed him full out.

Yes! She was finally here.

Sadly, even great kisses had to end, and eventually they separated to realize a dozen flashes had gone off and that Edward was still pushing through the throng. Mike was used to ignoring them, but Tori wasn't. She shifted uncomfortably in his arms, and he was forced to set her down. But he didn't let her go until he whispered into her ear.

"Not a word, okay, honey? Not with the press around. I've got a limo waiting just outside. Do you have luggage?"

She stilled for a moment and then nodded. He felt the dip of her chin as she squeezed him again just before letting go.

"The roses are for you," he said. "The jersey's for your father."

"They're beautiful." Then she looked up into his eyes. "Dad's got the flu. That's why he isn't here."

"Is he okay?"

"He's a cheap traitor, but I'll explain later." Her eyes searched his face. "You shaved off your hair."

Right. With the game tomorrow, he'd razored everything off this morning. He rubbed his bald head, feeling awkward. "Do you miss it?"

"There's nothing about you that isn't wonderful. Hair. No hair. You're still you."

God, she made everything in him ease. He would have said more, but Edward was elbowing his way forward, leading with his massive laptop which was slung over his shoulder. The words "big electronics, little dick" flashed through his mind, but he didn't let it show on his face. Edward was offering his hand and Mike took it gently though he wanted to crush the man—hand and all.

"Mike. Why didn't you tell me you play for the Knicks? I had no idea."

No shit, idiot. "Edward. What are you doing here?"

He opened his mouth, but then hesitated. "Honey, would you mind getting us a cart?" He shrugged off his laptop. "This thing is heavy."

Tori glanced at him, then back at Mike. He shrugged. Obviously Edward wanted to talk to him alone. So Tori leaned down and grabbed the laptop case before heading toward the carts. Fortunately, Mike was faster. He snagged the case off her slender shoulder and pulled it away.

"You don't need to carry that," he said.

"Oh. Thanks," she said, a soft smile in her eyes.

He'd carry a thousand laptops for that smile. He watched her walk away then, the shift of her hips in those jeans, the tight bottom that fitted so perfectly in his hands. And while his eyes were still on her sweet body, he passed the laptop back to Edward.

"Don't make a woman half your size carry your shit. What kind of man are you?"

"She's not half my size—"

"Edward, there are reporters here." He said that not to warn Edward, but himself. If the man kept talking, he was likely to punch the idiot and that would not please his bosses. And even worse, the press of people had blocked his view of Tori, so he had to shift his full attention to Edward who was awkwardly adjusting the laptop back on his shoulder.

"Okay. Right. Reporters. Look, I just wanted to say thank you."

Last thing he wanted was Edward's thanks, but he nodded as they started to move toward the luggage carousel. Sadly, the man didn't take the hint, but kept talking.

"It happened just as you said it would. The meathead left—early—and she was right there for me to console. I was worried in the first week. Never seen her so sad. But I got her back into her research. She's got this new idea about studying sports mythology." Then he paused and looked back at Mike. "Probably 'cause of you, huh?"

Ya think? And had the dickwad missed that kiss from Tori or was the poor little man wading that deep in denial?

"Anyway, all it took was a few coffees, a cookbook to say I was sorry, and a movie. Simple. You were so right."

Mike felt his insides hollow out, but he kept his voice even. "So you're back together?" He didn't want to believe it. Especially not after that kiss. Meanwhile Edward kept blathering on.

"Do me a favor: play well tomorrow. I'm going to propose at halftime."

He looked at the bastard. The clueless idiot who was

about to win a woman he didn't deserve. Jesus. "So she never told you who the…the meathead was?"

"Nah. I didn't let her talk about him too much. Said he was in the past. That she had to think about her future. She's with me now all because of you." He punched Mike lightly on the arm as if they were buddies. As if the bastard had a fist larger than a shrunken plum. "I can't thank you enough. I almost lost her, and now I'm going to marry the girl of my dreams."

"She hasn't said yes yet," Mike grumbled.

"She will," he spoke with enough confidence that Mike wanted to deck him. Then the guy made it worse. "You were right. I was too cheap with her. So I've made up for it with a diamond big enough that even you would marry me."

Which was all kinds of wrong. Especially since Tori didn't care about money or diamonds. Unless Mike was wrong. Which was a possibility since the woman of his dreams was apparently about to marry a prick with a big-assed diamond.

"There's mine!" Tori called from to the side. Damn it, he'd been so absorbed in *not* killing Edward that he'd lost track of her. But there she was, angling her way forward to a suitcase that was so quintessentially her. A ladybug suitcase. Hard case, bright colors, and it made everyone around them smile.

Then she gestured to a mammoth black thing. "I think that's yours, Edward," she called.

Good for her. She made no move to grab it for him and when Edward looked at him, he was too busy grabbing Tori's ladybug to help. Which left Edward to haul his heavy-assed thing off the carousel and look like a weak-muscled pansy. Petty? Sure. But Mike was in no mood to be magnanimous.

Then it was time to turn around and head to the limo. Except, of course, they had to get through the knot of seven journalists all asking the same round of questions:

"Who's the girl?"

"How's your shoulder?"

"Any thoughts about tomorrow's game? The Toronto Raptors are looking good."

Waving them off had become second nature to Mike, but Tori's eyes were wide as she looked at them, then back at him. Her question was obvious: should we talk?

He shook his head and pushed them through. Sadly, he'd forgotten about Edward. If it was one thing he'd learned early, it was that the man didn't know when to shut up. Mike had just made it to the electric doors when he heard the douchebag start talking.

"My name's Edward Burk and that's my girl Tori. We were lucky enough to meet Mike when he was recovering from his injury in Evanston. We're good friends and of course we're especially excited about tonight's game."

The game was tomorrow, dickhead. Fortunately, Mike was a big enough man to spin around, shoulder aside two paparazzi, and then grab Edward's arm. As soon as he latched on, he hauled him bodily forward.

"Not another word," he said into Edward's ear.

"But—"

"Shut. Up."

"My suitcase!"

Oh fuck. The idiot had dropped it. He looked at Tori and pointed to the limo. "Right there. Now." So much for seeing her face light up when she stepped into the vehicle. He'd made sure to have it stocked with her favorite beer.

Now Edward would get to see that face, but there was no help for it. He'd for damn sure not leave the bastard there to talk to the press. So he shoved Edward toward the car then went back in to reclaim the heavy-as-shit suitcase. Fortunately, that wasn't a problem for him.

He did pause long enough to give a stock phrase to the press. Something about looking forward to showing the fans just how recovered he was from his terrible shoulder injury. The bosses loved it when he said something to draw more people to the game. And since they'd been playing up his dangerous rotator tear, he was doing his bit to support the cause.

But as soon as he could, he ducked away and had to run for the damned limo. Security was waving it on. So much for being a superstar in his hometown. Fortunately, the driver Sammy knew his job. He braked and let Mike climb in, reporters on his heels. Then Mike slammed the car door and looked for Tori.

She was there, looking so pretty with the roses on her lap. Her eyes were sparkling as she held up the beer. It was a microbrew from a guy in Evanston.

"How'd you get this?"

"A credit card and Fed Ex."

She grinned. He reached forward and popped open the top for her as the limo lurched into traffic.

Edward grabbed a glass. "Tori's been telling me about her new love of beer. I'm all for trying new things."

He held out his glass, but Mike ignored him. Tori was already drinking from her bottle, her lips cherry red. He was mesmerized enough to miss his phone ringing, but she heard it and gestured with her beer.

"One of your legions of fans?" she said, grinning. "I knew you were famous, but I've never had to dodge the press like that before."

That was nothing, but he didn't bother telling her that. Instead, he glanced down at his phone and cursed. "It's Coach. Your plane was late, and that threw off the schedule." He'd begged her to come a day earlier, but there was some faculty something or other that she couldn't get out of. He understood. He really did, but that didn't make him any happier. And now he had team stuff to do.

"I'm sorry, Mike. You didn't have to pick us up—"

"The hell I didn't." He took a deep breath. "Look, I've got team stuff this afternoon, and then a media press-the-flesh thing tonight. I got you passes to get in—"

"We'll be fine," she interrupted.

Damn it, he didn't want her to be fine. He wanted her with him. "Tori—"

But she was talking to the driver. "Take Mike wherever he needs to go. Then you can drop us off afterward."

"You'll be there tonight, right? Sammy will pick you up." He wanted to be a dick and "accidentally" forget to add Edward to the guest list, but that was too mean. He wanted to stay friends with her even if nothing else was possible between them. And that meant being nice to the dick who didn't deserve her.

"Of course," she said.

"Wouldn't miss it," Edward added.

Mike didn't curse the bastard out, but he did glance that way. "So how is it that you ended up taking her father's seat?"

He started to answer, but Tori interrupted. "He paid my father to get sick."

"What?"

"Damn it!" Edward cried. "He wasn't supposed to tell."

Tori rolled her eyes. "Paid him to catch the flu."

Edward huffed out a disgruntled breath. "Negotiated like his life depended on it. He's a lot smarter than he looks."

Tori grimaced. "Dad wouldn't tell me how much, but—"

"I understand," Mike said, his voice dropping. Not in threat. More like frustration. "Edward wanted to make this a special trip." Just like Mike had.

It took him about two breaths to get his head on straight. Edward wanted to play big man on the town this weekend? Well he was gonna lose that particular game. This was New York City and Mike was a mega-star here. And Mike wanted to spend it with Tori. "So the media thing ends around ten. I thought afterward you could come by my place. We could talk. Have some beer."

Tori's eyes narrowed. Worse, her excited expression slipped. "You have a game tomorrow. Don't you have curfew or something?"

Oh right.

"And a system?"

The damned system. For the first time in his life, he was considering throwing it away. He could sleep with Tori tonight, and maybe the sex would boost his play. Lots of players claimed...

He cut off his thoughts. Maybe that worked for other guys, but a night in sexual antics had only ever weakened his play. Being sated and low on sleep made him fat and lazy on the court. And he had to play well tomorrow. It was important to come out strong and give the fans a good show. Important to prove to the coaches and Mr. Dolan that he hadn't lost a step. And important to his own peace of mind. This was his life.

So he nodded. Reluctantly. "Yeah, early bed for me. But you can keep the car. Sammy will take you wherever you want to go."

"That's a great idea!" Edward said with a grin. "We'll have an awesome night."

Fucking great.

Chapter Eighteen

Tori was speechless. And way out of her element.

She knew Mike was a superstar but hadn't really processed exactly what that meant.

They were at the night-before party, and he had made a beeline straight for her as soon as she and Edward had arrived. He'd smiled at her, looking at her the way he had back in Evanston. Part hunger, part amusement, and all what she loved about him.

Except, of course, he was clearly stressed. There was a haunted look in his eyes and an annoyance every time someone tugged on his sleeve. Not surprising, really. Someone was always tugging on his sleeve. But then he smiled, added a little swagger to his motions, and got on with the business of being a superstar.

She'd come here hoping to get a private word with him. She wanted to explain about Edward surprising her at the airport. She'd been furious, but unwilling to make a scene. Besides, it was her father who had sold her out to her ex.

Also, she wanted to tell him that she understood. It was

going to be hard for her, but now more than ever she saw how all-consuming his job was. The journalists at the airport were the tip of the iceberg. Reporters had followed them to the hotel and everyone wanted to know about that kiss. She'd promptly canceled her room and begged a couch for the night from an old friend who now taught at Columbia University.

But that wasn't all. Within an hour of landing, reporters started calling her cell phone. Mindful of Mike's advice, she didn't say anything beyond "no comment." But they were persistent and she ended up turning off her phone rather than go crazy with it ringing constantly.

This was Mike's element. Sure, she saw the tension in his shoulders, but everything else about him was smooth. He played the part of a humble superstar athlete to perfection. And yeah, she knew he was both, but taking the right note with the press was a balancing act that she hadn't a clue how to master.

Just as well he wasn't in love with her, she thought. She might be able to learn how to say "no comment" with panache. She could probably be taught how to smile and be on his arm without being a detriment to his career, but it would be hard. It would take time away from her research. And…and it was a lie.

It would be hard, but she wanted to learn it. She wanted to be with him and would do just about anything—even media training—to stay with him. All these mental games about how she didn't want to take away from her research were just that: games. She was trying to soothe the wound that Mike didn't want her like she yearned for him. He had his career and his system, and for the first time ever, she had an inkling of just why it required constant vigilance to stay on top of his field.

"You're amazing," she murmured and was surprised when he turned to her as if he'd actually heard her words.

"What?" Mike asked. "Jesus, I can't hear a damn thing in

here."

She smiled and shook her head. God she wanted him so bad her chest hurt.

"Just another hour, baby. Then we can blow."

"What about curfew?"

He shrugged. "I haven't seen you alone for five minutes."

God, she wanted it, too, but weren't they just fooling themselves? He was never going to give up his career to be with her. Maybe she could wait ten years, but God, that was a painful way to live.

Her throat tight, she reached up to touch his face. Just a touch and in it she tried to convey all her wishes. "You've got a big day tomorrow," she said.

"I've got time for you."

She shook her head. That was the whole problem. "You're paid a lot of money to focus just on basketball. We'll have time after you win."

"Tori—"

"Mike!" It was the booming voice of the Knicks' owner. "I was just telling Art here that…"

Mike cursed under his breath, but she pushed him toward his job. "Tomorrow," she said.

Then she slipped away.

•••

Halftime and Mike wasn't just in a foul mood, he was ready to hurt someone. It didn't matter that this was his big come-back game. That the Madison Square stadium was full or that everyone was cheering for him. Unlike other games, he wasn't high on the publicity or excited for the first game of the season. Instead, his shooting sucked and now the Knicks were losing. He'd been snarling at his teammates, curt with the media, and playing too aggressive and would soon get into foul trouble. And why?

Because he hadn't been able to talk to Tori since she'd arrived. She'd slipped away from the party before he could grab her. Her cell went straight to voicemail. And worst of all? He'd called the hotel and found out she'd canceled her room reservation.

So she was shacking up with Edward, and he was one bad pass away from climbing into the stands and decking the man. Yeah, they'd arrived too late for him to talk to them, but early enough that he got to see the bastard's grinning face as he put an arm around Tori in those first row seats he'd gotten them. Three steps to the side of the court and he could put Edward on the floor.

But that wouldn't win him Tori, so during a time out, he'd grabbed the closest team publicist. She was a sweet girl who was a little starstruck, so he got her to give Edward and Tori the grand tour during halftime. No proposal was going to happen before he got a chance to talk to Tori. And by talk, he meant plead, cajole, and seduce her into dumping the idiot.

But while the halftime show was still going on, Coach took him aside and ripped him a new one. This was why he had a system. Tori was distracting him. She was making him crazy and he was playing like shit. So maybe he needed to let her go. Because right here was case in point of why he never dated seriously while playing basketball. He was losing it. Big time.

Which meant it was time to focus. Forget Tori, forget whatever the bastard Edward was going to do. He was going to focus. "It's done," he told Coach. "I've got my head back. I swear."

Which might have worked if he'd done it in the first quarter. But now they were starting the second half and Coach didn't believe a word he said.

"You're benched until I'm sure your head's out of your

ass."

Or out of a woman.

So Mike sat on the sidelines and adamantly refused to look behind him at Tori. He didn't talk to her. Didn't smile at her. Didn't think of her.

All he focused on was the game. Pure and simple. The game.

And his system.

The end.

Chapter Nineteen

Tori was miserable. Edward had been an annoying jerk the whole morning. Breakfast at Tiffany's meant he gave her bagels (his favorite) as they stood outside Tiffany's and he talked about jewelry.

She was sore from her night on her friend's couch and Mr. Thinks-He's-So-Romantic was making her stand in the drizzle eating food she didn't like while looking at jewelry she didn't want. What the hell was wrong with him?

She asked him exactly that, but he ducked her question and took her to his next special stop: the Museum of Modern Art. At least he'd gotten that right. She loved the museum, but not before Mike's big game. She'd wanted to talk to him before he started to play, but she didn't want to distract him. So her thought had been to show up at the stadium in case he wanted to see her. But she couldn't do that with Edward dragging her all around the city.

She should have just ditched him and done what she wanted, but he was trying to be especially solicitous. He had been since they'd reconnected after Mike left. Didn't mean she wanted to spend her life with him, but they had a history, a shared language, and…and well this morning, she was trying to encourage his good behavior.

But now it was the end of halftime. They'd had a lovely tour of the stadium where she never caught so much as a glimpse of Mike, and she desperately wanted to duct tape Edward's mouth shut. He'd done some research into the game of basketball and was trying to impress her with his knowledge. In truth, he just sounded like a blowhard, and though she had a pretty high tolerance for that, he'd gone well beyond even her acceptance.

Then Mike was benched. That was bad enough. She knew enough about his game to know he wasn't playing well. There were any of a thousand different reasons why that could be happening—his shoulder, the pressure, hell, even his shoes might feel wrong—but she knew he'd blame her.

It was his damned system, and if this was the result of having her watch him play, then she could understand why he wanted her out of his life.

She tried to catch his eye. She wanted to just smile encouragingly at him, but he wouldn't look her way. His body radiated tension and she had to accept that this was the way life was for him. Which meant she'd never come see him play in person again. Not if it destroyed him like this.

Which is when she saw the coach walk up to him on the sidelines. Tori had a front row seat to the angry, clenched expression on the man's face. She couldn't see Mike's face, but saw him stand and shake out his muscles. He was nodding and clenching his hands open and closed.

Five seconds later, he was back on the court.

She jumped up and cheered as he went in. She and a few hundred thousand fans, but it did no good.

Oh shit.

He was still playing awful. Even with her limited

knowledge, she knew he wasn't supposed to double-dribble and then a few minutes later get called for traveling. It was after that last call that he finally looked at her. Their eyes met and she saw defeat in them. Anger, frustration, and defeat. And it was aimed at her.

Slowly, she sat back down into her seat.

Well. Here was his system in glorious action, and now she understood that even if it wasn't true for other athletes, he clearly believed in it. A self-fulfilling prophecy if there ever was one. Which meant she and he were done. There was no way they could make this work. Basketball was too important to him.

She didn't come back to herself until Edward started tugging on her hand to get her attention.

She blinked and looked at him, startled to realize he was down on one knee before her.

"I was going to do this at halftime, but I didn't get a chance. So even if Mike loses this game, I want it to hold some happy memories for us."

Tori frowned. "What the hell are you talking about? Mike isn't going to lose…" Her voice trailed away as he pulled out a ring box and opened it.

Jesus. The skinflint had actually gone whole hog. That was one big honking diamond ring. She'd never wear something that big. It would forever be catching on things and weighing down her finger. And she'd be terrified some desperate student would mug her on the way to her car.

"Edward, this is not the time…"

"I know. It should have been months ago, but I'm doing it now. Tori Williams, will you marry me?"

•••

Traveling. Mike barely restrained himself from cursing out

the ref and getting himself called for a technical. Fucking hell. He ought to have his head examined.

He glanced over at Tori. He couldn't help himself, which is when he realized the truth.

He was in love with her. Full out in love.

Whether she was with him or not, he wanted her. He ached for her. And he was going to play for shit whether she was with him or not.

Fuck.

The game started up again and he tried to focus. Cole intercepted. Good for him, but his friend and teammate couldn't make the lay-up. Rebound and Mike had the ball. But then, out of the corner of his eye, he saw Edward go down on one knee before Tori.

Now? He was proposing now with just over three minutes left in the game? Yup, there he was with a ring box while Tori gaped in shock.

Mike called a time out.

He didn't even think about it. He called it and was rushing over to the stands where Edward was saying some nonsense.

To the side, the players, the coaches, even the fans were screaming at him, but he was completely trained on Tori.

"Don't do it!" he bellowed. "Tori, damn it, listen to me!"

She looked up and double blinked. Her eyes filled with tears, and he almost stopped himself, terrified that he was about to hurt her. Jesus, he was so confused, but he had to tell her. She had to know the truth before she accepted the dickhead's proposal.

"Mike—"

"I love you. Don't marry him. I want to work this out. I want you, not… not basketball." There he'd said it. She was more important to him than his career, and damn it, the words felt *right*.

"But what about your system?" she asked. "Your career?"

"It doesn't matter. If I'm going to play for shit because I love you, then that's the way it's going to be."

"Oh no," she said, pushing to her feet. Edward still had hold of her hand, was still offering up his ring. But his mouth was open and he started making noises.

"Tori! I'm proposing marriage here!"

"No."

She wasn't looking at Edward, her eyes were on Mike. And damn, it was loud in here. Out of the corner of his eyes, he saw the TV camera aimed right at them. And the coach and about a dozen more people running straight for him.

Oh shit, he was going to get fired.

"Tori," he begged. "Who are you refusing?"

She frowned then looked to the bastard. "Edward, I'm sorry. I told you a month ago at lunch and again last week, but you refused to listen. We are not getting back together. That means we're not getting married."

"But—"

She turned her back on him. "Did you hear that, Mike? No way am I marrying him. But, I'm also not going to be the reason you lose basketball."

"It doesn't matter. It's love—"

"Forget that." Her face took on that stubborn edge he adored. "I love you, too, but here's how it's going to work. You've got to prove that love makes you better."

She loved him. She loved him! Jesus—

"Wait—" said Edward. "You love him? Is he the guy from the summer?"

Tori rolled her eyes. "I told you on the plane I was still hung up on my summer guy."

Then she grabbed Mike's face, not to kiss him but to glare into his eyes. "Now listen to me. You're going to do five three-pointers and win the game. Do you hear me? And then I'll marry you."

He blinked at her. "What? I'm...what?"

She kissed him hard on the lips. "We'll work things out, but only if you make five three-pointers. Got it?"

The sweat was burning his eyes, and his mind was racing. "There's only three minutes left in the game." Then he gestured at the TV camera. "And you've just told everyone what I want to do."

"Three minutes and twelve seconds. Go get 'em."

He clenched his hands. Now was not the time for pie-in-the-sky plans. "Tori, no one could do that!"

"Then if you do, you'll know that our love is stronger than any damned system."

Behind him, the whistle blew. Shit, he was out of time. Five three-point shots? In three minutes and twelve seconds? No way. And yet...

She was standing there, love shining in her eyes.

"Do it for us," she said. "I love you."

She loved him. For her—for love—he could do anything.

So he ran to his place and played. He played as if his life depended on it, and in this case, it very well might. Because if he didn't pull this out of the crapper, she wouldn't marry him and he'd be fired to boot.

In-bound pass. Foul. Crap. But at least this time the penalty was on Toronto, not him. Fine. In the background, the fans were going wild and the coach was screaming at him. His teammates looked grim, and a couple shook their heads. But thank God for Cole. The Knicks' greatest rebounder gave him a thumbs up.

"I'm going to do this," he said to no one in particular. Or perhaps to everyone.

And then he took control.

First three-pointer rimmed and flew out. Fuck.

But Cole grabbed it out of the air and instead of going for the easy lay-up, he passed it back out to Mike. That was a true friend.

Mike shot and the ball went swish. First three-pointer down.

Toronto had the ball, but it was like Mike's feet had wings. He was faster than he'd ever been in his life, and he stole the ball right out from them. He started dribbling back to the basket and suddenly he was surrounded by Raptors. Well, they hadn't taken long to decide to triple-team him.

He was considering his options when he heard her voice. Hadn't a clue how he could zero in on her over all the noise, but he heard Tori cheering. And in his head, her screams translated to: I love you. Do this for us.

So he did. He faked left, then leaped up and shot.

It wasn't pretty. It banged on the backboard too hard, but somehow it dropped in.

Second three-pointer—check.

He didn't have the time to look directly at Tori, but his peripheral vision was enough. She was climbing over the wall with help from his teammates. At least some of the guys were smiling at her.

And then he saw only the ball.

The Raptors shot their own three-pointer and scored. Fuck. The Knicks would need every one of his baskets to win. That's probably why Coach hadn't benched him.

They had the ball, but the Raptors were sitting on him now. No way could he make the shot. But that left the others wide open.

Under two minutes.

He loved Tori, but he couldn't be completely selfish or stupid. So he leaped up and didn't shoot. Instead, he passed the ball to Cole. Two points, but it didn't help him win the girl.

Diving forward fast enough to steal the ball did. Especially since as soon as he got it, he pivoted and shot with his bad arm. Swish.

Number three—check.

Now Toronto was slowing things down. They weren't letting him close and they weren't going to shoot the ball. They could drain the clock.

Fuck that. He was winning Tori.

He made some stupid lunges. Desperate attempts to steal the ball. Ugly play, but it worked.

He failed miserably to get the ball, but there was Cole faster than any guy his size ought to be. A quick pass to Mike and he shot.

Number four—done.

Thirty seconds left on the clock. Score tied.

Desperate to get the ball, he fouled a Raptor shot.

Oh shit. He'd forgotten that was his fourth. One more and he would foul out of the game. Those were the rules.

Twenty-two seconds left in the game.

The Raptors scored on their free throws. Of course they did. Bad guys up by two.

Then he got the ball, shot and—

Missed. By a mile.

He was too anxious. Too needy for that last shot. He had to be smart. Basketball wasn't just about focus, it was about planning. About skills. And it was about finding a way no matter what—without being stupid.

But the clock was ticking down.

The Raptors weren't going to give up the ball easily.

He glanced at Tori, an apology in his eyes. He wasn't going to make it. There just wasn't enough time. She was standing on top of the bench. No other way to see or be seen. And when he looked at her, she thrust out her jaw in the most stubborn expression he'd ever seen. Then she dropped her hands on her hips.

The message was clear: Do it or else.

Fine.

He loved her. She loved him.

And he was a badass NBA basketball star. He was going to find a way. But the Raptors were too smart. They didn't let anyone get the ball.

Eleven seconds.

Eight seconds.

And then a stupidity happened. He'd seen it before, but not since high school. Players got so caught up in watching the other guys on the court—not to mention the fans, the coaches, the media, and the love drama playing out before them—that they forgot their own feet.

The Toronto point guard stumbled.

Cole and Mike both lunged for the ball.

The Raptor danced away, but not before tripping himself up. Not bad, but that was the opening they needed.

JR got the ball and started flying down the court. He was a good player and could have done it. He had a solid three-pointer himself. But in a move that surprised everyone, he bounced the ball backward to Mike who had just recovered from his lunge.

Two seconds.

Mike grabbed the ball.

Took two steps.

And shot…

Chapter Twenty

Go in.

Tori held her breath—as did everyone else in the stadium.

Go in.

Mike's shot had to make it. Sure she wanted to marry him either way, but this was about proving to him that he could do it. That he was stronger in love than out of it.

Go in.

Buzzer! The game was over, but not the shot. If it went in, then they won. Mike won.

Please go in the fucking basket.

Swish.

It was so perfect it took her a second to process it.

He scored! The fifth three-point shot and the game.

Holy shit, he did it!

People swarmed the court, but Tori had eyes for only one man and he apparently for her.

She didn't know if he shouldered everyone aside or if they parted for him. Either way, two seconds after the buzzer, he was lifting her up in his arms.

A split second later, they were kissing.

And kissing.

And drenched in something wet.

They both came up sputtering. Someone had dumped the water tub on them. But she didn't care.

He'd done it.

"Say it again, Tori. God, say it — "

"I love you. I want to marry you. You're done with your stupid system. Now we're doing mine."

He lifted his head, blinking the water out of his eyes. "Anything. Just marry me."

Coach came over, an evil grin on the man's face. "From now on, Giamaria, she's giving you incentive. And I'm going to tell her what it is."

He reared back. "Hell no, Coach. Her incentive is between us."

"Not that shit," Coach answered. "I'm giving you the goal. She handles the reward."

He could do that. He could... "So I'm not fired?"

Coach shrugged. "There might be a fine. Up to the boss. But if you two play the media right, you'll boost ticket sales. And that's always good."

Mike looked back at her. "That okay with you?"

"Okay? It was my idea."

That same media was even now pushing forward, cameras trained on them, questions drowning out everyone else.

He looked at her. "Answer with the truth, Tori, because it's going out to the whole world. You'll marry me?"

She grinned at him. "Yes, I will."

"What about the rest? Your job? Your house? Your life? I don't know that I can get traded to the Bulls."

She blinked. "Oh. Didn't I tell you? I stayed last night with a friend who teaches at Columbia. He says there's an opening in the religious studies department coming up next year."

"You're a shoo-in."

She laughed. "Call it my goal." Then she arched her brows. "So what's my incentive?"

"Courtside seats for the rest of my career?"

"Hmmm. I don't know. I just renovated this house in Chicago."

He grinned. "As much hot sex as you can stand?"

She shook her head. "Baby, I've been in charge of my own—"

"Right." No need to force the networks to bleep out her words. "How about this? I swear to love you, to honor you, and to cherish you until death do us part."

Her face lit up, and damn he was once again caught by the beauty of her whole being. "I do."

Epilogue

"Mike, look at this." She'd nabbed a book off a nearby kiosk in the bookstore café. It was placed strategically so that anyone at the nearest tables could grab straight off the shelf.

Her husband of two months looked up from his latte and a book on successful kids' after-school programs. "What?"

She held up a book on mountain climbing complete with a very happy couple on the side of a mountain. The woman even had a toddler strapped to her back.

Mike frowned as he studied the title. "What am I looking at? The colors? The people? The sexy climbing boots?"

She laughed, the sound unrestrained. "I was thinking about the kid, actually. Would you take a child mountain climbing with you?"

He winced. "That young? I don't know."

"But they look so happy."

"Because they're getting paid to look pretty." Then he lifted the book out of her hand. "If you want to try mountain climbing, I'll give it a go. But if I fall and break something, you'll have to tell Coach."

She shuddered. She'd learned over the past year just how much of a hard-ass the Knicks coach was. Turned out the owner was much more of a pussy cat. At least as long as Tori stayed within the guidelines of what her media training had emphasized and Mike's play continued to dazzle everyone. Fortunately, he was having no trouble with that part.

"Actually," she said as she took the book back. "I was thinking about the kid."

"He looks happy, too."

She laughed. "Yeah, he does." Her gaze lifted to Mike's. And right then her life changed. The words spilled out without thought, but once said, she didn't regret it. "So you want to try it?"

He stilled. Then he spoke quietly and carefully. "Try having a baby? Tori, are you telling me you're pregnant?"

She shook her head. "Definitely not. At least I don't think so, but I want to be." With her job at Columbia locked down, everything in her life was on track. And even more surprising, she found she didn't have to pretend to be a ditz anymore. If she wanted to be left alone, she just said it and then a security guard made sure it happened. That was one advantage to living in the media spotlight. There was usually security around to make sure she had privacy when she needed it. Plus having a huge superstar husband helped in that area, too. Mike made sure she had the space she needed to do whatever her heart desired.

Which meant she had room in her life for a baby. She had room for a whole parcel of Mike's babies. "So…do you?"

"Yes."

"Yes?"

"A thousand times yes!"

She nodded, her mind already making plans. He'd made a convert of her on that score. "Fine. Coach says you need to steal the ball six times tomorrow, and then we can start trying."

He blinked at her. "You talked to Coach about kids? Before me?"

"God, no." Hell, she hadn't thought of it in such concrete terms until just this moment. But that didn't lessen how much she really, really wanted this. "He just said you have to steal the ball. That you're getting a little slow on your feet."

"The hell I am!" But he smiled as he said it. Lately, he'd been much more accepting of the idea that he was aging. And though he'd never played better, she had good hopes that when the time came, he could step away from the spotlight without too much trauma. Especially if they had something else to occupy his time. Like a wife who wanted to spend more time with him. And a child or three…

"Okay," she said with a smirk. "He didn't say you were getting slow. I added that part. But if we're going to have a baby, you've got to keep bringing in the money."

He snorted. "Tori, we've got plenty."

"Not if you're going to single-handedly revitalize urban ghettos." Then she leaned forward and kissed him slow and sweet on his lips. She'd meant to tantalize him, but found herself completely revved and wondering how long it would take to get back to their penthouse apartment.

"We need to get home, right now," he growled.

She'd like that, too. A lot. "Six steals."

"If I make seven you're going to let me cuff you to an office chair."

She grinned. "Deal."

And then they said it together, because they were always that in sync.

"I love you."

About the Author

Kathy Lyons is the fun, contemporary side of USA Today Bestselling author Jade Lee. She loves sassy romance with lots of laughter and sex. Spice is the variety of life, right? Okay, so maybe two kids, two cats, two pennames, and writing over 40 books has messed with her mind, but she still keeps having fun.

Check her out at www.KathyLyons.com.

Or hang out with her sexy historical half, Jade Lee. Titled heroes with dark secrets are Jade's passion. Especially when they fall for women who add more than just spice to their lives.

Find her at www.JadeLeeAuthor.com
Facebook: JadeLeeBooks
Twitter: JadeLeeAuthor

Find love in unexpected places with these satisfying Lovestruck reads...

THE ARMY RANGER'S SURPRISE
a *Men of At Ease Ranch* novel by Donna Michaels

Army brat Kaydee Wagner's grandfather needs help repairing his home, so she steps up. She has no clue what she's doing, but surely she can wing it? Wrong. Help arrives in the form of troubled former Army Ranger Leo Reed. After a very...*wet* incident involving deadly dance moves and a wayward sink hose, their clothes hit the floor faster than a stack of tile. Leo doesn't want forever. Kaydee only wants right now. Their white-hot attraction should be the perfect arrangement...until hearts get involved and Kaydee discovers she's pregnant.

THE BEST FRIEND INCIDENT
a *Driven to Love* novel by Melia Alexander

Stacey Winters's best friend Grant offers her a window into the male psyche—and sets the bar high for her future Mr. Right. But then she accidentally crosses the friend zone and kisses him. Grant Phillips doesn't do relationships. "No attachments" is his hard and fast rule. There's only one exception: his best friend, Stacey. But now that he knows how good it felt to kiss her, felt the addictive slide of her body against his, Stacey Winters is indelibly stamped onto Grant's brain—and not just as his friend.

Breaking the Bachelor
a *Smart Cupid* novel by Maggie Kelley

Matchmaker Jane Wright just made a bet—she'll find the "perfect" match for Manhattan's hottest confirmed bachelor, sexy-as-sin bartender Charlie Goodman—Jane's ex-lover—or lose her company. Charlie doesn't want to see Jane's business fail. He just wants a little revenge. Determined to prove that chemistry *always* beats compatibility algorithms, he plans to drive Jane crazy with desire, then walk away. And Charlie's plan is working.

Tell Me Something Good
a *One-on-One* novel by Jamie Wesley

Life, and love, is too short to take seriously—a fact radio sportscaster Tate Grayson enjoys rubbing in uptight radio host Noelle Butler's face. But when he tells his listeners men shouldn't get married, she's all too happy to call in and yank the silver spoon out of his overprivileged mouth. Their heated on-air arguments are a hit, but when they're forced to do a joint show for two weeks, they must pull the struggling radio station back from the brink or they'll lose their jobs. Or worse, their hearts.

www.ingramcontent.com/pod-product-compliance
Lightning Source LLC
Chambersburg PA
CBHW030309200626
46816CB00002BA/820